THE NEW WATER

THE NEW WATER

Roy Jacobsen

English translation
William H. Halverson

Peer Gynt Press
Columbus

Distributed by the Ohio State University Press.

Originally published in Norway as
Det nye vannet
© 1987 J.W. Cappelens Forlag a.s.
Roy Jacobsen

Library of Congress Catalog Card Number:
96–71723

ISBN 0–9645238–1–7

Designed and typeset in Goudy Oldstlye and Copperplate
by John Delaine Design & Production.
Cover illustration: Howard Sortland.

Printed in the United States of America.

The paper used in this publiction meets the minimum requirements of
American National Standard for Information Sciences—Permanence of Paper
for Printed Library Materials.
ANSI Z39.48–1992

Publication of this book was made possible by a translation grant from NORLA.

9 8 7 6 5 4 3 2 1

THE NEW WATER

1

Jon woke up when the gun fell out of his hands and crashed to the floor. He had been sleeping with his clothes on, sitting in the chair. Through the curtains he could see that another gray day was dawning. It was four o'clock.

He stood up, stretched stiffly, and went to check on Elisabeth. The food was still on the table, untouched, and her bed was empty. He turned on the lamps in the living room and started the video camera.

"I've been waiting for over six hours," he said peevishly. "You were supposed to be here at ten. Now it's . . ."

He stopped to think about what he wanted to say. He yawned. Fragments of a dimly remembered dream flitted briefly before his eyes. "I'm going hunting," he said, holding the new gun up in front of the lens. "Here it is. Six shots, telescopic sight, walnut. It's Finnish. Bet you'd like to know what it cost, wouldn't you? Ha ha. But that's a secret."

When his mother was living, *she* was the one who got to see everything new, both the things he bought and the things he made. Now it was his sister, Elisabeth. They lived here together, in the house their grandfather had built. It had been constructed over a period of time—a plank now, a stairway then; it was never really finished—depending on how the fishing went year by year. Jon had lived here his whole life. He held the gun to his shoulder, squinted through the telescope, and pulled the trigger.

Then he went into the kitchen, wrote a note, placed it in a basket on the table, put on his jacket, and left.

It was autumn. A thin haze hung over the broad marshland. A shudder rippled through his numb body.

He walked southward along a sheep path, with the sea in the west and the bluish-black mountains rising like a shadow against the sky in the east. Half an hour later he stood at the north end of the tarn. He waded across a narrow stream and crept the last few meters on all fours. From a small knoll he saw the rushes on the other side, the shoreline beyond, and the lush, green meadows that had only recently been put to the plow. He crept farther, to the top of another knoll, and squeezed into a small opening under the bushes.

Ten minutes passed; then the geese were there. Up through the haze on throbbing wings, as always. They made a wide arc in the sky, flying southward, then westward, out over the sea, beyond the horizon, then back again—first audible, then visible—landing at last in one of the meadows on the other side. There were more than twenty of them, and the distance was perfect, about two hundred meters.

He picked out the biggest one, the lookout, and studied it carefully. He moved the cross hairs slowly up the motionless breast, along the arched neck, let them rest for a few seconds on the piercing dark eye, then down to the belly and back to the eye again, up and down in slow, controlled S's. "As a rule the lookout stands still," he thought to himself, "usually in silhouette. It makes a beautiful target, but it's always old and tough, almost unfit to eat."

He moved the cross hairs to the closest young bird, zeroed in on its multicolored breast, and fired without hesitation. A wing flew skyward, quivering and white in the gray half-light. As the sound of the shot rolled across the marshes the flock took off and disappeared with the echo.

Jon was warm. He walked around to the other side of the tarn and inspected the dead bird. There was an almost invisible spot among its feathers where the bullet had gone in and a red clot where it had come out—leaving a big hole, to be sure, but nothing like the craters his old rifle used to make. He held the wings out full length and thought to himself that Elisabeth would never understand how good a marksman he was. He had told her over and over again, but how can you *tell* somebody about the delicate precision between finger and trigger, about the well-oiled machinery that ticks off the seconds until just the right moment, the impact of the bullet hitting the target, the stillness, and the ensuing crackling sound that rushes off in all directions? You can't. And besides, Elisabeth was totally lacking in imagination. She was a teacher at the local elementary school. She corrected students' essays and wrote articles for the newspaper—and made Jon lonely with her long and complicated love affairs and the endless stream of friends who dragged her off to meetings and committees. All she had left for him was a few lousy lunch hours, and often she didn't even have that.

He repeated the hunting exploit at a meadow farther south. New wings and new echoes. His clothes were wet in the front, and he was sweating. His ears were filled with the contented quacking of grazing geese. He got his third one at the edge of a big thicket of willows. The fourth one he stumbled upon in a creek bed.

Suddenly it was broad daylight and quiet. The light hung heavily over the marshes, the wary birds had vanished, presumably flying out to one of the smaller islands.

He headed home by way of Long Lake, and as he picked his way along the steep slopes of the mountains on the south and east sides of the lake he kept an eye on the two divers who were working on the new water system. The reservoir lay a few hundred meters up in the mountain. The aqueduct came down through the ravine; it was to go through the lake and northernmost marshes to the center of the village.

The two men were in a boat, near land on the other side of the lake. Dressed in bright orange outfits, they were leaning over the edge of the boat and tugging at a cable. A little farther north, where the ravines began to give way to meadows, lay the ruins of an old farmyard. Jon went there and lay down to watch what they were doing.

Bracing the gun against one of the rotting floor timbers, he could see them clearly through the telescopic sight. The divers were talking loudly to each other, and their voices carried well in the quiet surroundings. The cable emerged from the pearl-gray surface like a slimy serpent. Evidently they were in the process of removing the moorings from the old aqueduct.

Suddenly a shadow loomed beneath the bow of the boat and they stopped tugging. They also stopped talking. One of them fell backwards into the boat with a shout and the other one turned away.

Holding the gun as if to shoot, pressing his eye against the eyepiece, Jon saw that the shadow in the water resembled a human body. For several minutes it was as if his brain had ceased to function. He fell down between the timbers, down among the thickets that grew wild between the moss-covered walls. He could hear water falling drop by drop from the stone face of the mountain, and he could hear the rustle of the birch leaves in the gentle breeze. He could see the mighty arch of the heavens, the gulls soaring over the sea in the distance, the mountains—and yet, it was as if he himself were not there.

Then he was up again, and so were the divers. They were standing in the boat, speaking quietly to each other. In the depths beneath them he still saw something that looked like white skin, an arm with fingers clearly visible, and a dark waving motion that undoubtedly was hair.

He laughed softly, shook his head and blinked his eyes. The scene did not change.

6

When the divers were done talking it over, one of them began pulling carefully while the other maneuvered a sandbag up on the railing—a weight to hold the waterpipes down. They rowed in a semicircle around the figure, fished up the mooring on the other side with a boat hook, cut it off on either side of the hook, fastened the ends together around the sandbag, and dropped the whole thing back into the water. He saw it all, every little movement. And the shadow vanished.

There followed several minutes of motionless silence. The divers sat in the boat and smoked. Then they rowed off as if nothing had happened.

Jon snaked his way through water puddles and wet grass on the back side of the ruins. He crept past the stones and up into the birch forest, out of sight.

He ran home.

His note still lay untouched in the basket on the kitchen table. His spit tasted like salty iron, his clothes stank of marsh water and sweat. As long as he had been running he had had something to do. Now he just stood there, deeply agitated.

"You're not here now either," he said reproachfully into the video camera. What kind of a sister is that to have, away and busy all the time?!

He flung the geese and the rifle down angrily and started walking around in a circle in front of the video camera. His confusion made him cry. He felt threatened: something was after him.

He kept it up for half an hour. Then he sank into the chair and went to sleep, awoke again a few seconds later and began to undress.

He looked at himself in the mirror, looked out at the new day dawning—perhaps one of autumn's clearest. He looked at the geese and the coagulated blood on the homemade table. He looked at the new gun, at the video camera. And at the house. Sure enough, with or without Elisabeth it was all there, as it always had been. Everything. He could sleep.

7

By the time the front door opened a little later that morning, he was asleep. Her footsteps in the hall, the familiar sound of Elisabeth undressing, making sure that the fire was burning in the fireplace, the fetching of slippers from under the bench, the soft sound of felt on the worn stairsteps, and at last the faint click of the closing door—he heard none of it.

2

She was sitting on the edge of his bed when he awoke. The sun was shining at an angle through the south window, so he knew it must be late afternoon.

"I couldn't let you sleep any longer," she said in a motherly tone of voice. "Besides, what are you doing in my bed?"

He looked around. First at the room, then at her—carefully, to see if she had changed again. For Elisabeth was always changing. She had been in the casting ladle since the day she was born, had flitted here and there in response to every passing fancy. Now she was past thirty and almost out of reach, he thought—he who had been the same his whole life, had liked the same things and had always been faithful to the noble things in life.

"I heard you cry out," she said. "Did you have a nightmare?"

"Yes . . ." He couldn't remember for sure.

She had a swollen mouth, red cheeks, and shining eyes—as she always did after spending a night with Hans. He looked at the long hair that was sometimes braided or combed, sometimes rolled into a bun under a cap or kerchief. It had always been long. Now it was disheveled and hung in big clumps over her round shoulders. He thought it was like a halo in the sunlight, and that she was like an angel. Why was she so determined to move away from the island? Why couldn't she settle down here—like her parents, like her grandparents, like Jon?

"Now that the municipality is getting water we won't have to move," he said.

"But we can't live on water," she laughed.

He reminded her of the angry debate about this water that had filled the pages of the newspaper for several years. A debate that she herself had participated in—she and Hans and the other teachers.

"I don't think you ought to take it so literally," she said. "And don't you remember how cold it was in the winter? Ice cold all the time, no matter how much wood we put on the fire. The house is too old, too poorly insulated . . ."

He wanted to revive an old quarrel about renovating the place, but she cut him off by saying that it would cost a fortune. Besides, soon there wouldn't be anyone left out here. She was referring to her friends—her fellow teachers and school administrators—who were ready to abandon both the school and their mortgaged homes.

"But we *live* here," he said.

"Relax. There are over three months left, and by that time you will have changed your mind. You'll like living in the city, I guarantee it. You'll have things much better there than you do here."

He didn't believe it. He had been to the city. It was awful there.

"I *mean* it," she said. "By the way, those were some fine geese. Did you get them by the tarn? We used to skate there when we were kids. Do you remember?"

"I won't leave."

"Of course you will. Get up now. I've made some food."

"Have you looked at the cassette in the video camera?"

"No, is there something there for me?"

He went down, took it out of the camera and stored it among the others on the shelf. Some two years of his life were recorded on those tapes. Mainly isolated messages to Elisabeth, mild reproaches and stern rebukes. She never looked at them.

He found some clothes, dressed, and went out to the kitchen.

"What nice birds," she said as she poked at a wing with a shudder. "But shouldn't we hang them up out in the shed?"

It was the *little* changes that he disliked the most, the slow, gradual wearing away—erosion, as it was called in his illustrated nature books. Things you couldn't see until it was too late to do anything about them. These plans to move, for example. An innocent vacation trip down south was all it had taken to give her fantasies about a new world and a better climate. It was so cold here, it was dark half the year, and it rained all the time. "Besides," she had said in her most political tone of voice, "the population base is disappearing. It's not like it was when we were young, with fishing and trapping and farming and bustling life. Things have come to a standstill. The municipality is going broke." Even the prospect of the new water hadn't been enough to restore the old optimism.

He hung the geese in the shed, sat down at the table and watched her as she chattered away about love and men. Some lines had appeared in the white skin around her eyes. That was erosion too. The nights with Hans were obviously not all fun and games. Between the wrestling matches there presumably were rancorous discussions about a possible divorce, about that possessive wife of his who wouldn't be able survive on her own, and about the children—of which there now were no less than four. The rest of the world wasn't exactly the way she wanted it either: it resisted virtually every attempt she made to improve it. People were either ignorant or deceived; in any case they didn't know what was best for them. "That includes me, too," he had thought to himself out of habit when he first began to think along these lines. "I will be a big burden to her too."

"I need a husband," she said. "There's no doubt about it. Otherwise I get crabby and cross, and I don't like that. Do you like me when I'm crabby and cross, Jon?"

No, he didn't like her when she was crabby and cross. He didn't care much for the subject either.

"I want some coffee," he said, pushing his plate off to one side. He was sure that after a night like the one she had just had she would do anything for him.

Otherwise she could be more obstinate and start a long harangue about who should do what around the house. For Jon liked to do whatever he was in a mood to do, but she was forever talking about

11

what he *ought* to do. Among other things, he ought to cook his own coffee, especially in view of the fact that she didn't drink coffee but lived healthily on herbal tea and warm milk. But Jon didn't know how to cook coffee—when she was away he turned the water heater up to three and used instant coffee—and he didn't want to learn. He wanted her to do that for him, just as his mother had done.

Elisabeth cooked coffee.

But he had an itching sore on his knee, and his body ached after his long outing. He had the feeling that someone was calling to him across a field, trying to give him an ominous but important message that he couldn't quite hear; and while Elisabeth was cutting the cake and getting cups on the table, he went upstairs and sat for a few minutes in his mother's old room, where everything was still just the way it had been when she died. But the memories gave him neither peace nor an answer, for they were old and belonged to another world.

"I think I'll take that job with the divers after all," he said impatiently when he came down again. The old pipes that were being hauled up from Long Lake were going to be cut into shorter lengths and used by the highway department as drain pipes. The civil engineer had been trying for a long time to find a man to do the job, and Elisabeth had nagged Jon about taking it. "You never do anything," she had said.

"Are you serious?" she asked.

Yes, of course he was serious.

"Wonderful. Will you go to Rimstad and tell him yourself, or shall I do it?"

"I'll do it myself."

She looked at him. "Are you afraid?"

The question was not irrelevant. Jon was afraid of everything new.

"Yeah, a little."

"It's nothing to be afraid of."

"No."

12

"It'll get you out among people a little."

"Mm."

He couldn't stand being out among people. He had three friends, and that was more than enough. In addition to Elisabeth there was Karl, the neighbor from the farm where Jon had lived when Elisabeth was at the teachers' college. And Nils, an old man who lived with his third wife, little Marta, on the small farm just to the north. Nils had been a childhood friend of Jon's grandfather, and their friendship had continued through their youth and beyond as they worked together year after year on the fishing boats. As a young boy Jon used to go there every day to hear Nils's incredible stories, but now senility had so ravaged the old man's brain that nothing remained except a few scattered memories of childhood and the most firmly established habits. If you put a tool in his hands he could perform a simple task—tar a boat, for example, or mend a fishing net.

Jon made it a point to get him away from the kitchen table and steer him down to the shore. There they could sit on a stone and feel the wind in their faces, and perhaps the spray of the sea when the weather was bad. The path was steep and uneven, and they had to cross a footbridge. But old Nils had been there before, and with Jon's index fingers nudging his ribs to show him the way he always managed it. Once there, Jon whisked the old man's cap off and stuck it under his bony rump as he sank down on the stone. The wind rumpled the few strands of hair that remained on the balding head, and a contented smile stole over the otherwise expressionless face.

"A sea gull!" he might say, enraptured—as if this flying creature were today, here and now, revealing itself for the first time ever on the face of the earth.

"That's not a sea gull," Jon would say. "That's a duck."

"A duck," said the echo.

Why did he keep on doing this, long after the stories and the companionship had ceased? Out of habit. Because it made people in the community say something good about him, say that he was a nice boy. Plus the fact that he sometimes enjoyed having an idiot to take care of.

But there was another reason too. Life is strange, he sometimes thought. After eighty years on the planet there's nothing left but an empty brain in a useless outer shell.

And he found that thought at once both saddening and heartening. In a single moment of insight he could see before him life's great mystery, see clear to the other side, and see that there was nothing, and that everything enroute to that nothingness is transitory.

Yes, one might just as well be a sea gull. It wakes up, flaps its wings, lays an egg, and dies. That's all. Jon could carry on the most challenging conversations with himself.

"What are you going to make of yourself, Jon?" the world might ask.

"Make of myself?" he would then answer contemptuously. "One doesn't have to make anything of oneself. We'll just end up here, sitting on a stone by the sea."

"Are you going fishing this winter, Jon?"

"Why should I? Look at that fellow. He went fishing his whole life, and look where he is."

"Go and see a doctor, then!" (That was Elisabeth's voice, no doubt about it. It meddled in everything.)

"No!"

Nils had told the most wonderful stories, lived the most industrious and normal of lives, and still he ended up a lunatic.

So, in a way, Jon's trips to the sea with the old man gave him the right to live as he did. They gave him respite from the wrinkled brows. The admonitions vanished, and the scruples slumbered.

Now things were different.

"I feel so strange," he said. His hands were trembling and the coffee didn't taste good.

"That's because you don't take your medicine."

In Elisabeth's world there was a remedy for every injury and for

14

all suffering. If you suffered nonetheless, it was either because you hadn't taken enough of the appropriate remedies or because you didn't know how to use them—in which case all you needed was more information.

"That's not the problem," he said irritably.

He picked up the new gun, rubbed some invisible specks of rust off the barrel, aimed at a lamp shade, and tried to enjoy the compact solidity of a perfect piece of handiwork.

"What is it, then?" she asked. "Does it have anything to do with me?"

"No."

"You don't think I'm neglecting you, then?"

"Yes."

"Well, then, is *that* the problem?"

"No. Why doesn't he ever come here?"

"Hans? He doesn't like the fact that you run around with all those guns. He's afraid of you. Do you want me to invite him, maybe?"

"No, no."

It was the voice calling to him across the field, ominously calling. He understood all of a sudden that everything could be destroyed and disappear—Elisabeth, the house, the whole island. This was the warning.

"I'm going to talk to Rimstad," he said. He picked up the grocery list that she had set out for him and left in the hope that the sight of the island and its daily life would have its customary soothing effect on him.

He dropped in on Karl, who took him out to the barn to show him an inflatable whore that he kept there so his wife wouldn't see it. It had come in the mail the day before, and if Jon kept his mouth shut he could try her out sometime. He stopped at the store, where he bought the things on the list and exchanged a few words with the owner about an old bill for some boat equipment. Then he went down to the freight room by the wharf, where one of the coastal steamers was tied up for repairs, and to the post office to buy stamps and send off an order for a pair of hunting boots that he had seen advertised in a newspaper.

For the most part, things were as usual. Petter, from North Island, sat in the sandbox by the gas station and wrote down the same license numbers he had written down yesterday. Little Rune, who was too much of a bully to go to preschool and too dumb to go to school, was, as usual, playing in the ditches with his red pail. People greeted him and talked amiably—except for Gerda on the moped, who looked at him with the same malicious, slanderous, venomous look that she had always given him.

Perhaps beneath the surface, invisibly, a fuse lay sputtering, but there was no upheaval to be seen, scarcely even any erosion. The bus proceeded on its usual route with its milk cartons, passengers, and mail sacks; the mound of silage in Karl's meadow was exactly one wagon-load smaller than yesterday; the air smelled of fertilizer and fish oil; the wind blew in your face, and it was a life with no earthquake. Just a life; a long, thin thread running through an unwashed embroidery of habit and monotony—as he wanted it and as it always had been.

Finally he went to the administration building to see Rimstad, civil engineer in the Technical Services Department. Rimstad wondered why Jon had changed his mind, but Jon himself didn't know the answer to that question. All he knew was that he felt drawn toward the lake. Yes, of course the job was still available. Who else would want to stand out there in the marsh and saw off plastic tubing for a few lousy crowns an hour? Ha ha!

As Jon was on his way home it started to rain. A strong westerly wind churned the sea and abruptly covered the island with dark clouds. Jon put the groceries in the entryway and ran down to the shore to secure the boat. The wind was already so ferocious that he had all he could do to get it out of the water. He pushed sawhorses under each side of the boat, tied it down as tightly as he was able, and crawled under some driftwood on the sheltered side of the boat-house. This was a place where he had spent countless hours of his life—thinking, feeling unhappy, or just enjoying the elements.

The green ocean pounded the stony shore with crushing mountains of water as it always had done. The eider ducks huddled together in the crevices on the reef. Rain-squalls blew through the cove, one after another. But still the sense of foreboding remained—less clearly, perhaps; suppressed, more muted, but still there—throughout the entire storm.

3

Jon had been standing and waiting for a long time, waiting in the darkness among the trees. The sounds of merrymaking streamed through the open windows of the community center and across the parking lot, which was filled with cars and motorcycles and boisterous crowds of unruly young people. As usual, he had waited too long, and he was beginning to lose his courage. He was wearing a nice jacket and his best pants—and muddy boots, to be sure, but out there at the bottom of the hill nobody was sober enough to notice them anyway.

Then he saw Karl standing alone by one corner, and headed directly for him. They looked at each other, but Karl was in no condition to say anything. His red eyes stared out of deep, moist sockets, and something wet was constantly moving either up or down through his gullet. It was Jon who did most of his haying and slaughtering, Jon who fetched his sheep from the mountains each fall. And it was also Jon who had dug most of the miles of ditches that Karl owned out in the marshland.

Karl flexed the muscles in his neck, threw his head back, and yanked a bottle out of his inner pocket. It had no cap and was nearly empty.

Jon took a swig and continued on toward the doorway.

Two young men stopped him at the door. They said something to him, but he walked on without answering. Once inside the dance hall he bought a cup of coffee, managed to avoid engaging in small talk with the girl in the kitchen, and took up a position by one of the vertical timbers. No defeat so far.

The fellows who had stopped him at the door came over to him again. They operated a salmon farm on North Island. Jon had known them since they were babies. They always said the same things and had smiled at his misfortunes as long as he could remember.

"Hi, Jon," they said as they flaunted their powerful shoulder muscles. They had big motorcycles and leather jackets, and they wore kerchiefs around their necks. They had so many girls that they didn't even bother to look at them until three o'clock in the morning. And the salmon farm was the fattest golden goose anyone had ever shot on that island. Jon couldn't stand them.

"Hi," he answered curtly, looking away from them. He fixed his eyes on the dance floor and the band, which consisted of four young people from the town on the mainland. A man stepped on a beer bottle and fell down with a crash, taking two chairs and a young girl down with him. The girl screamed and crawled away from his groping fingers. Jon laughed out loud.

"Have you run away from home?" one of the boys asked.

"Yeah," said Jon.

"Whatcha doin' here then?"

"Don't know."

"No, 'cause you're not exactly an expert dancer."

They laughed and talked about Elisabeth's boobs, but Jon didn't hear them. He made it a point not to say much when he met these two. Now he surprised them by asking a question.

"Who are those two guys at the table over there—the ones with Kari and Gerd?"

"Those two? They're the divers who work out at Long Lake. So what? And when are you gonna cut off that long hair? It ain't the style any more."

Jon had always had long hair. He wanted to be fashionable, but as soon as he tried he just became more ludicrous. Besides, the old stars from Nashville still had long hair, and so did the English heavy-rock musicians, Jon's heroes.

He left his tormentors, walked over to the divers and stood quietly by the table until they noticed him. Kari asked what he was staring at.

"Are you drunk?" she shouted.

He looked directly at one of the divers.

"You're not from around here," he said.

"That's right," said the man, looking him up and down as the girls giggled. "We're just here to do a job. But you—you're from here, aren't you?"

Yes, Jon was from this area.

"I can tell by your uniform. It's obviously local."

He put his hand on Jon's string tie and understood from the girls' giggling that this shy oddball was the local idiot.

He was a fairly handsome man in his mid-thirties, short of stature, with an angular, dark face, black curly hair, and lively brown eyes that appeared to take in everything that was going on. There was a pervasive darkness about him—something rat-like, thought Jon, who often characterized people in terms of their similarity to animals. Elisabeth, for example, was a swan—a slightly overweight swan.

He asked if it wasn't strenuous, working out there in the marsh for such a long time.

"It sure is," said the diver loudly. "But now, fortunately, we're almost done. Another couple of weeks and then . . ."

His face expressed vividly how happy he would be in a couple of weeks when they could leave this place.

"*Fortunately?*" said Gerd peevishly.

"No, no. Of course we'd rather stay here forever—wouldn't we, Paul? With you girls."

His companion nodded, and Jon noticed that both of them had mud under their fingernails and wore wedding rings. He could tell

20

that they shared the opinion of most strangers regarding this island—that it was a wasteland, an anteroom of death. It rained every day so you couldn't see from one house to the next. The only reason to be here was to earn money, lots of money, and in the process take full advantage of the scant opportunities for relaxation that were available.

Jon said without further ado that the marsh contained a secret. And both men stopped laughing.

"What do you mean by that?" the short, dark man asked sternly.

"Nothing," said Jon, returning the stern look. He had been preparing for this moment, and he knew how to make use of silence. It was up to the divers to make the next move. What happened instead was that Kari jumped in to try to remedy the tense mood, saying that Jon never meant what he said.

"Isn't that true, Jon? Sit down and have a drink."

Jon took the drink standing up, a hefty swig of yellow home brew. He poured a little in his coffee as well, but continued to stare into the diver's face, waiting. It was obvious that the man didn't like the fact that he was sitting and Jon was standing. He cleared his throat and pushed his chair back a few inches.

"Someone has gone *down* there," was Jon's next move. Another short sentence, again without explanation.

"What do you mean, 'gone down'?"

"Gone down! Gone down in the marsh! Are you scared?"

"Scared?"

The man got red in the face.

"Why the hell should I be scared? Are you crazy, boy?"

"He's talking about an old legend," said Kari. "We still live in the stone age out here. People believe in fairy tales. They believe in ghosts, and premonitions, all kinds of crazy things, just not in God . . . So does Jon."

The diver looked from her to Jon. He drank a swallow of home brew and peered out over the dance floor. Jon noticed that his companion, Paul, who had kept his hand on Gerd's knee all this time,

21

now removed it. There *was* something fishy going on here. And Gerd smiled uncertainly.

"I don't believe in fairy tales," said Jon. He remained standing and continued to stare intently and inquiringly at the diver. And now the man became irritated.

"What kind of fairy tale is this?" he shouted. "Is this nut going to stand here all night and speak in riddles, or what?"

"It's a fairy tale about love," Kari giggled reassuringly. "About *unhappy* love. There's a story in the chronicle of local history about a handsome young man who used to live out that way, on the farm by Long Lake. He fell in love with the pastor's daughter, and she with him. He did everything he could to win her, but the pastor wouldn't hear of it because the man was so poor. Finally he agreed to let them marry if the man could meet the conditions he set down, namely . . ."

"All right, all right," said the diver. "I don't need the whole story . . ."

"It was a *girl*," said Jon in an attempt to keep the conversation on the right track.

"Oh, my aching back!" said Gerd. "It wasn't a girl. It was the *man* that went down. He wasn't able . . ."

"A girl," said Jon.

"A man!"

He looked the diver in the eye.

"What do *you* think?"

"Me! How should I know anything about that?"

Kari threw her head back and laughed uproariously.

"He knows *one* foreign word," she said exuberantly. "Right, Jon?"

He raised his hand to signal her to be quiet, but she was not to be stopped. "Say it, Jon. We'd all like to hear it."

He mumbled something inaudible to shut her up, but the divers, happy for an opportunity to break the tension, started to laugh. Suddenly he had lost control of the situation; they were no longer scared. Paul's hand was back on Gerd's knee, and the rat eyes were

22

just as lively and self-assured as before the conversation began. It was a party, people were dancing, there was booze in the white cups. Jon understood that he had blown his opportunity.

He left the table and sank down in the chairs where the wall-flowers were sitting, next to two homely girls who were trying to prove that they didn't mind sitting there exhibiting their loneliness. He was starting to get drunk. Behind half-closed eyelids he tried to figure out a new way to get at the divers, but to no avail. Somebody poured some more home brew in his cup. A few minutes later he passed out.

The next thing he knew he was in a crowd of people by the door. He was standing now, walking out into the rain with everyone else. The party was over. As he reached the steps the diver with the rat face came and took him by the arm.

"Those girls are crazy," he said with a diffident smile. Then he took a different tack. "I have to talk with you. Do you have time?"

The diver walked a few steps into the darkness, stuck a cigarette in his mouth, and fiddled with some matches that wouldn't light.

"Care for one?"

"No."

He threw them away.

"Why did you come specifically to me with that story?"

Jon wondered vaguely what story the man was talking about. As far as he could remember he had played all his cards and they were no good; in any case it was past midnight. He wanted to leave but the diver was holding him back.

"Answer me," he said curtly.

"Let me go," said Jon.

"Did you hear what I said?"

Anger made the furrows in the rat face even deeper, and Jon realized that the man was drunk. Moreover, he was a stranger here and he was acting foolishly.

"Did you hear what I said?" he repeated much too loudly. "You idiot!"

23

An ominous silence fell over the jostling crowd. It was no longer necessary for Jon to tear himself free. He belonged here. Yes, he was an outsider, and maybe an idiot too, but he was the community's idiot and nobody else's. One of the young men from the salmon farm staggered in between them, stuck his face a couple of inches from that of the diver, and asked if there were any idiots here.

The stranger looked at the crowd in the glow of the yard light, saw the island's youth here assembled as a wrought-up and inebriated multitude, and realized that he had been naked all evening long.

"Are there any idiots here?" the young man repeated menacingly. And when the diver still did not answer, he calmly took hold of his jacket pocket and hung on it with all his drunken weight until the jacket tore and he went rolling end over end in the gravel.

The crowd loved it.

Laughing derisively, he got back to his feet, threw his arms in the air in a gesture of victory, and savored the moment. A beer bottle came flying out of the darkness and hit the diver just below the eye.

Jon got himself down to the birch grove to watch the rest of the incident from a distance. The two young men from the salmon farm took turns fighting with the diver, half seriously and half in fun, egged on by the rest of the mob. The mood got more and more boisterous until Kari and Gerd came out and saw what was going on. They knew the language. The diver was rescued, and the crowd jeered as the two couples ran down the road into the safety of the night.

The racket began to die down. For awhile there was some talk about where the party might continue. Couples and individuals crept into the shadows and disappeared, motorcycles roared, and overfilled cars glided one after another out of the parking lot. Finally the light was turned off and the doors were closed behind the last reeling party-goer.

Usually Jon took an interest in who went home with whom, and who didn't go home at all but disappeared into a barn or a hayloft to write yet another secret chapter in the island's unending chronicle of hidden reality. But not tonight. He stumbled through the grove, followed an old wagon trail down to the shore, and walked home to the familiar sound of gently lapping waves.

He was alone tonight too. That was surprising, for Hans's wife usually didn't work on Saturdays, and Elisabeth had said she would stay home.

He started the video camera and sat down in the chair.

"I have seen the divers," he said. "I have talked with them, too. They're scared."

But he didn't say why. Instead he chided Elisabeth for not being home. "You promised!" he insisted.

When Jon died—and that could happen anytime—the video archive would supply the bad conscience that this self-centered sister of his had so craftily avoided all these years.

Little by little, as he found words for his loneliness, the self-pity made him feel almost as if he were choking. His body heaved with uncontrollable sobbing. The image in the monitor showed him with wet hair clinging to his face; he looked pathetic and mistreated, worse than in his darkest moments.

"I don't take my medicine any more," he shouted, "and you know how it hurts. You promised to help me!"

He let himself be carried away until it struck him with painful clarity that what he was sitting here and saying was the truth: he really *was* the most pitiful creature on God's terrible earth. He ran up to his room and turned the stereo on full blast.

"I'm still a child," he shouted. "I'm so little. And there's nobody to take care of me!"

He looked at himself in the mirror. Nice jacket. Like hell! He tore it off and threw it in the closet. And *those* pants? Who the hell went around with shit like that today?

He threw open the window.

"I'm miserable!" he bellowed frantically into the darkness.

And it helped. "I'm miserable!"

25

He closed the window, turned down the stereo, and sat quietly in the chair, spent.

"I'm crazy," he realized as he looked shamefully at himself in the mirror.

He felt himself to see if he had any desire for a girl. Usually after a party he felt a rabid desire. But no, not tonight. He smiled.

4

It was cold and raw on the morning near the end of September when Jon left the house to begin his first day of work at Long Lake. The sun hung like a yellow egg floating in the haze, and there was no wind. To the west was the sea, brooding and still. The first snow of the season looked like mildew marking the dividing line between the mountains and the deep blue sky. It made a crunching sound as he walked.

The divers were already at work when he arrived. They stood out in the water, bent over, working with the end of a black plastic pipe. One of them was holding a welding device, the other a screwdriver and a coupling. Only Paul was wearing his diving gear.

A compressor droned away at the edge of the camp, the crew shed smelled of fresh coffee, clothing and equipment were scattered about in the heather. A blackened area marked the site of a bonfire. Nearby were stacks of pipes, pipe couplings, and concrete weights.

Jon walked over to the boat and sat on the gunwale. It was rat-face who saw him first.

"You here?" he said, perplexed. Jon held his hands up as if to say, "What does it look like?" The divers looked uncertainly at each other, then rat-face waded ashore. The screwdriver he was carrying looked like a weapon. Jon stood up.

"I'm going to work here," he said. "I'm going to cap pipes."

"The hell you are. I don't want you here. Go home!"

Jon didn't go.

"I *mean* it," said the diver. "Get me somebody else."

27

"There isn't anybody else. Just me."

"That's bullshit. The island is full of young people without jobs."

His face was flushed with anger. The yellow remains of a shiner still ringed his right eye, and his upper lip was swollen. Jon looked away meekly so as not to make the situation any worse than it was.

"Is this a plot?" the diver bellowed. "I ask for a man, and of all people who do I get but *you?*"

By this time Paul had also come ashore. The two of them walked off a short distance to confer, and when rat-face came back he was more composed. He dried his hands on a rag and nodded toward a jeep that was parked on dry ground a short distance up from the shore. They walked over to it.

Rat-face took an electric grinder out of a wooden box and plugged it into an outlet on the compressor.

"So Rimstad has sent you," he muttered. He handed Jon a reel holding an extension cord, and they unwound it in the direction of a pile of old water pipes lying in a creek bed about fifty meters away. "You. Just you."

"Yes. My name is Jon."

"Do you know how to use a power saw, Jon? One like this?"

"Yes."

He kicked a length of pipe into position.

"They're soft as butter. You cut off the ragged ends, like this. Then you cut it up into 6-meter lengths. That board there is three meters long. Use it as a measuring stick: two of these, then cut—so."

He wound the piece he had just cut around two wooden crates and threw the rest of the piece into the thicket on the other side. Jon took the power saw, cut off a length of his own, and wound it around the crates.

"I don't like this," the diver said pensively. "There's something wrong with you."

"What's that?"

"I don't know. You stink. Why do you want to be here, really?"

"To work."

They looked at each other.

"Okay," he said calmly. "Work, then. And when you're done, get the hell out of here."

Rat-face rejoined his companion and Jon began to cut pipes. They had been lying on the bottom of the lake for about ten years and were covered with foul-smelling slime and green seaweed. Water squirted out in every direction, and the putrid odor of scorched plastic and raw sewage filled the air. Sometimes it was so overpowering that it made him vomit. Jon was used to working alone, but this he did not like.

He gave himself short breaks now and then, and during these periods he climbed the hill to see what the divers were doing. They were never working with anything except the welding equipment and the pipe couplings, and there wasn't the slightest hint of anything secretive about what they did. By lunch time he was beginning to lose his patience.

"I'd like to learn to dive," he said as they sat around the fire eating.

"There's no reason why you couldn't do that," Paul said nonchalantly. Paul had red hair, freckled pink skin, pale blue eyes, and a little white moustache. He was taller than his companion, also younger and more muscular. Jon couldn't think of a suitable animal name for him at the moment, but it had to be something that lived at the seashore.

"So you can go diving in the ocean and catch fish?"

"No. So I can dive here."

"Here?"

"Yes."

"What good would that do?" asked rat-face, whose name was Georg. "There's nothing here but mud. You can't see anything."

"So?"

"The point is to *see* something, isn't it?"

"Yes, I suppose so."

"What are you really after? Can you tell me that?"

He couldn't. And it was Paul who once again rescued the situa-

29

tion by saying that he had seen a sign at the post office about a diving course that was to be given at the local school. "You could start there," he said.

"After we finish eating you come with us," Georg said gruffly. "We're going out in the boat to pump air into the rest of the old pipe."

"Okay."

"We want to bring it ashore."

Jon nodded.

The narrow lake stretched all the way to the ravine at the foot of the craggy mountains, where the sun's rays had now melted the white flakes. The mountains were over a thousand meters high, and Jon was probably the only person in the world who had ever climbed them to the top. He had sat like a cowboy atop the highest and sharpest peak, where a misstep in any direction meant certain death, to show the teachers and other students on a school field trip that he wasn't afraid. He *was* afraid, for deep within the mountain he sensed life and movement. He could see into three counties, could see where the ocean ended and the sky began. He shivered from both cold and exhilaration, for he was a microscopic detail of an enormous being, above the clouds; the longer he had sat there the clearer it had become to him that the mountain was alive.

He remembered nothing of the trip back down the mountain and was never able to tell anything about the experience, either to brag or to report his honest impressions. In his weakest moments he was not even sure that he had ever been up there. The mountains constituted a kind of oasis in his memory, a place to seek refuge whenever circumstances compelled him to think through life's deeper questions. "Something happened that day," he could say to himself, without going into the details. "Something happened."

The rest of the day was spent out in the boat. Jon operated a big reel with a pressure hose, Georg handled the oars, and Paul was mainly under water.

Jon was no more content here than he had been with the pipes, for he was keenly aware that now the two adversaries were alone on a thin membrane between life and death. They might do something to harm each other.

"Why do you put up with people making fun of you?" Georg asked.

"I don't put up with it."

"Well, they do it anyway."

Jon shrugged his shoulders. "I know them," he said.

"Maybe you do," said the diver.

They were not more than a hundred meters from the spot where he had seen the shadow in the water. The ruins of the old farmyard were barely visible at the foot of the mountain; the divers couldn't possibly have seen him that morning.

"How can he work down there if he can't see anything?" Jon asked.

"He can see a little if he doesn't stir up too much mud—about so far." Georg held his fist about six inches from Jon's left eye. "It's a matter of moving slowly, *working* slowly, and knowing what you are doing."

Jon nodded.

He preferred not to look at the diver. He looked at autumn. Although huge flocks of geese were still flying about, and some seabirds still gathered on the stones in the sea, most of the birds had disappeared. Today there was not even any wind. And nobody ever came this far out into the marshland.

How can you stand living here, year in and year out?" Georg asked.

Jon didn't think it took much effort to live here. He just was here.

"If it weren't for the fact that we're earning big money," the diver added, "we wouldn't be here for a day. It rains all the time."

"Not today."

"No, not today. But we've been here five weeks."

31

Paul and Georg made their livings as fishermen and construction workers. Now they were here, now there; home and away and home again in haphazard confusion. Jon did not envy them.

The oars lay unmoving in the oarlocks as Georg rolled a cigarette and talked about those five long weeks on the island. It sounded as if he was talking only because there was so much silence around him. Jon listened to hear if it really was all that silent. Today, as always, the sound of the sea could be heard in the background. Now and then a gentle breeze wafted through the birch trees on the shore. And if you listened carefully you could also hear, ever so faintly, a brook that flowed over the edge of a cliff in the mountain and was transformed into white mist as it cascaded down the black ravines.

The shadow of a sea eagle appeared on the surface of the water. Jon pointed upward. Georg stopped talking, and both of them leaned back to gaze at the bird, which looked like a sail in the sky.

"That's how it is here," Jon said with a smile. And perhaps the diver understood what he meant, for he smiled too.

"I was up there once," Jon volunteered a few minutes later. "On the highest peak. It's one thousand and thirteen meters high. You can see everything—north, south, all the way to the mainland on a clear day."

He told about the class trip that he couldn't remember anything about, embellishing the story as he went along. The world was clearly visible from up there, exposed. Only on the farthest horizon were you in doubt about whether it was islands you were seeing or clouds."

"But *you* know what you see?"

Yes, because he knew this area. The islands, the mountain, every stone, every blade of grass. It was as if they were parts of his own body. "Some young people killed themselves up there once," he said. "A boy and a girl, as they were fetching the sheep from the mountain meadow in the fall. They got separated from the others during a storm and couldn't find their way down. The storm lasted for several days . . ."

"More bad weather," said the diver, "and more tragic stories. You seem to have plenty of both here, don't you?"

Jon took the hint and fell silent.

"He's fastening a plate to the end of the pipe," said Georg. "There's a valve in the plate. He'll connect the air hose to the valve. He lies completely still so he can see what he's doing. Understand?"

"Hm"

"When he's ready we'll pump air into the pipe so it will float to the surface. Then we'll pull it ashore with the winch on the jeep. And you'll cut it up into 6-meter lengths. Yes?"

They smiled.

"But doesn't the air go out the other end?"

"No. The last part remains hanging down, full of water, exactly long enough to keep the air from escaping."

Jon smiled again. Nobody was going to talk about the shadow in the water. This episode was like all the other secrets that the island hid away in a musty attic and only talked about when people were drunk. Elisabeth's divorce was a secret of that kind, as was also that miserable husband of hers and the current relationship with Hans. There were also a couple of questionable land deals on North Island, an unexplained grass fire that spread to the fish works, boundary disputes that never got resolved, children who never learned to read but were kept at home more or less in seclusion their whole lives. To be honest, he himself was one of those manifestations of bad luck, a burden to his gifted sister.

"Pay attention!" said Georg. "Reel out more hose."

Jon reeled out more hose. There were new instructions and he reeled it in again. Paul's orange diving outfit came into view in a cloud of mud and murky water. He clambered into the boat and pulled off his diver's mask. Georg started the motor, and as they moved slowly toward land Jon let out hose from the reel and rope from a coil in the bottom of the boat. Once ashore they connected the hose to the compressor and the rope to the winch on the jeep. The stinking pipe rose slowly to the surface, and they began to haul it in. The sandbags divided it into a series of clearly defined sections, making it look like a serpent slithering through the marsh, section by section. Jon cut it up into 6-meter lengths and stacked them up on the crates. And the work day ended, as naturally and unproblematically as any other day.

He walked home and stood briefly in the yard. He smelled boiled fish and burning wood, saw the dampness clinging to the window panes, heard Elisabeth moving busily about in the kitchen, and once again he felt the terrible fear that all of this was about to vanish. They were so vulnerable, it was so easy to do something crazy here—in a house at the top of the world, a house that at this very moment was bathed in the last blood-red rays of an exhausted autumn sun. He could only do what he had done during his school days when he didn't understand which principle the bright students were using as they put the right numbers in the boxes: he could only bow his head, hum a quiet tune in the privacy of his own soul, and wait for the bell to ring and set him free.

5

Jon had run all the way from Long Lake to tell Rimstad that the divers' compressor had fallen into the marsh. Then he stopped in the parking lot in front of the administration building and became totally confused. He saw several things at the same time, like pictures seen through many layers of colored film: two Danish hunters in green hunting garb were climbing into a four-wheel-drive vehicle, a tractor that he had seen many times before was standing there with its motor running, and through the big glass windows of the tax office he saw Lisa's father leaning over the counter. Jon hadn't thought of Lisa for several months; then he heard the Danish voices, saw her father, saw the familiar tractor, and he couldn't understand why she had been away, for she was his youth and had always been there. He didn't have *three* friends; he had *four*—and she was the most important one. She was the youngest daughter of the biggest businessman in the community. She was Jon's age, Jon's love—and the island's most untamable beauty.

He felt the rain trickling down his neck and remembered again why he had come. But why hadn't he thought of her? Was it because she had left him in the lurch and run off to Copenhagen to become a ballet dancer?

He ran the rest of the way up to Rimstad's office. Rimstad—a big, gruff man—sat behind the desk with his countless maps and rulers, and he got even gruffer as Jon gave his halting and breathless report about the compressor. They were going to move it. To save time they had used the jeep instead of waiting for a tractor. The

35

ground was wet and slippery from the rain, the vehicle began to slide, and they had to cut the cable so as not to lose the jeep as well. Georg had managed to throw a rope around one wheel of the compressor, and . . . well, there it hung.

The engineer turned away from the pile of papers with an angry curse. One more catastrophe in connection with that damned waterpipe! He summoned two road workers who were in for lunch, made arrangements to get a tractor and two more workers, and ordered everybody to meet down in the garage.

On the way out to the work site Jon had to repeat the story— but Rimstad only got madder and madder as Jon was unfocused and constantly lost the thread of the story because of the renewed memories of Lisa. Ballet dancer in Copenhagen? That was no reasonable way to continue a life that began out here. Here one became what one's parents were, or one became nothing at all. Jon and Lisa had grown up together, everybody knew that they belonged together. Through school, puberty, and confirmation they had each manned an oar in the same fishing boat, had worked side by side in the fish packing plant. They had the same enemies, the same tastes, the same dreams and desires—until she escaped from the claws of her tyrannical father and ran off to Copenhagen to become a dancer. Perhaps it was more like madness than like a fairy tale, but if you examined it closely it wasn't so very different from all the other anecdotes in the local chronicle.

The roads were slippery, almost impassable, and by the time they finally got there the compressor had sunk almost out of sight. Only the severed cable and a small part of the yellow engine housing bearing the municipality's name protruded from the oily surface of the water.

It was raining furiously. They stood there, all seven of them, on the edge of the marsh and stared. Rimstad swore and chewed them out. Georg had a stern look. He had mud on his face and a cup of cold coffee in his hand. One of the workers checked the little birch tree that was almost being torn from its roots by the tug of the rope. There wasn't much they could do here.

Georg, to be polite, suggested that he could go down and fasten a chain around the wheel; then they could try to pull the thing up with the tractor. All that came of that was that Rimstad called him an idiot and an irresponsible fool.

"We're not going to kill ourselves here too," he bellowed as he pounded on the rope, which looked as if it might start to unravel any moment.

"Okay. So what shall we do?"

"What the hell were you trying to do out there?" Rimstad shouted. "This will delay the project by several days. And where can we get another compressor?"

"In the city, maybe?"

"That costs money. This water project has already skinned us alive."

"Maybe one of the farmers around here has one," offered the man on the tractor, but Rimstad ignored him. His whole attention was on Georg.

"This isn't the first time you've screwed up, is it?" he said bitterly. "I was warned, both against you and against your firm. But I didn't have any choice. We don't have any choice out here. We have to take what we get, right?"

Jon was confused. The old merchant, Lisa's father, was somehow involved in what was going on here on the edge of the marsh. He was the island's financial backbone. He bought and sold every fish that was brought ashore, owned the biggest and best plots of land on which to construct school, administration, and other public buildings. He also controlled the new wharf that had been built to accommodate hydrofoils. Not to mention his workers and his children: three daughters with two different wives, and a son who left home and never amounted to anything—not a worthy heir, in any case.

"Okay," Rimstad broke into his thoughts. "What shall we do?"

"Stand here and look," said Georg crossly.

"We don't have time for that."

The diver looked at him coldly. Then he picked up an axe and cut the rope just below the knot. There was a slurping sound, a rush of air bubbles, and the compressor sank into the mud.

He turned his back to the others and began to discuss with the man on the tractor where they might be able to get hold of another compressor. They agreed to try a farmer who did some dynamiting on the side.

"Do as you please," said Rimstad as he was leaving. "Do whatever the hell you please. Just so the job is finished by the fifteenth!"

"This island is poison," mumbled Georg when they were alone. He got out of his coveralls, which were soaking wet, and disappeared into the crew shed.

Paul yanked Jon out of his daydreams and together they moved the Jeep up to firmer ground. Then they resumed the task of welding together the pipes for the new aqueduct, Paul handling the welding apparatus while Jon maneuvered the pipes into place and attached the concrete weights as the conduit floated out into the water.

His memory was a mish-mash. Now he couldn't even remember what Lisa looked like. Oh yes, he could remember some individual features—that she had freckles in the summer time, for example, and fiery red cheeks in the cold of winter; the long dark hair that she never cut, the slight squint in one of her big, dark eyes that sent a cold chill down his spine when they met. But the whole? The figure? He remembered that she could drive a car and water ski, that she could shoot a gun—not as well as he could, but well enough. Most jobs got done in a flash when she put her mind to it, and the men were crazy about her. But he couldn't *see* her.

It was over an hour before Georg came out again. In dry coveralls, but paler and with even deeper lines in his face than before. He looked like a man on the edge of a cliff. It occurred to Jon that the

38

divers had now been here for over seven weeks, with nothing but work, loneliness, and mud night and day. He knew what it was like from having worked in the fish business: you work and work, get little sleep, and dig yourself in deeper and deeper. Finally something snaps and someone begins to fight, has an accident, or takes off. Then things usually calm down for a few days again. But the sun continues to rise nonetheless, and the world struggles along one way or another.

Here things went differently. It appeared that the two coworkers didn't have to exert themselves to make progress. Jon noticed that they never looked at each other. They just worked. Georg had taken over the job of attaching the weights, and Jon put the pipes and sleeves in place in the clamp in front of the welding apparatus. The divers exchanged roles without a word every half hour. They worked swiftly and precisely, with no unnecessary motions—not faster and faster, like amateurs do when they think they are accomplishing something—in the same controlled tempo all the time, in a rhythm of maximal effectiveness; and Jon, with his breathless sprinter's mentality, understood that there would be no fight here. These men knew each other. They had been pressed to the wall before and knew how to convert inner turmoil into work and production.

"We'll keep on," Georg said at four o'clock as he handed the pipe wrench to Paul and took over the welding apparatus. At five he said it again. At the five-thirty role shift they smiled wanly and stretched their backs as Jon went to the crew shed to get some halogen lamps. They exchanged roles for the last time at seven, and a little before seven-thirty there were exactly enough lengths of pipe left to keep Jon and Paul busy the next forenoon while Georg went to the wharf to get another load.

Then Lisa was there again, as he plunged his hands into a bucket of lye water behind the crew shed and saw the yellowish fluid dissolve the mud from his skin. He remembered her as she was in the photographs in the drawer at home, in the first picture when he opened his eyes in the morning. What lies would she have to resort to today to get away from her father and daydream with Jon on the heath between their homes? They met half way, saw each other from a distance of a mile or more—little chessmen who popped up out of the knolls and became coconspirators in the island's biggest secret. He had read a book about them once, and it ended happily, for it never ended; the two lawbreakers were just together, together, together.... He missed her. God, how he misssed her.

6

Rain again.

Jon stood in the darkness outside the school and stared into the gym, where a ballad singer was entertaining an audience of twenty or so, mostly teachers and school administrators. Elisabeth was there, and most of her friends: the new minister, with half of his scout troop; Rimstad's wife, who was a physical therapist at the old people's home; and way in back, by the basketball hoop, was Hans, a good distance away from his lover.

"A lousy liar," Jon thought to himself. A fawning camel who above all else wanted to be friends with the students who didn't like him.

Hans had come to the island ten years ago looking as if he were on a hike in the mountains, with parka, rubber boots, and a full beard. Now he had a wife and kids and a new house, the beard was gone, and he generally wore corduroy slacks and a leather jacket. But he still had that same untrustworthy look.

He had been one of the zealots pushing for the new aqueduct. At first nobody would listen to him. But he was a biologist, and he had gone around on his own and collected water samples from the private wells and had flung them on the table to prove his point to the authorities and the local dumb-heads. He had said that this mud had the bacterial content of a whole barnyard and an oxygen level well under half of what was permitted, that nobody could live on such stuff without suffering ill effects. And slowly people had come over to his side. First colleagues and friends, then the experts in the

41

directorate and those who had something to *gain* by it—the businessman Sakkariassen, for example, and the entrepreneurs and the biggest farmers. When the proposal finally was put to the municipal council it passed by an overwhelming majority.

In the first row sat a woman in her late twenties. She was the one Jon was waiting for. A fashionably dressed city woman with black stockings, a ton of jewelry including a bracelet that no doubt rattled erotically, and coal black hair done up in the latest style. She had a camera in her lap and a scratch pad on which she was not writing. She was a journalist from the city paper, the one to which Elisabeth often sent her "Dear Editor" letters—as Hans did also—and occasionally a poem about the weather and scenery as well.

When the concert was over, and most of the audience had run through the pouring rain and gotten into their cars, Jon emerged from the shadows and offered to help the journalist with her umbrella. She stepped back in alarm, so he let his hands dangle at his side to show that he meant her no harm.

"You frightened me," she said, holding her hand to her chest, but she handed him the umbrella anyway. He coaxed a jammed latch into the groove and opened the umbrella. This encounter had been carefully planned, each sentence rehearsed—and now he couldn't remember a word of it.

"He sang about peace, I suppose?" he said in a conversational tone of voice as he nodded toward the singer, who was just getting into the pastor's car to be driven to the ferry.

"Yes," she said laughingly. "There aren't many who care to listen to that sort of thing nowadays, are there?"

Jon had a rather strained love life. For the most part it was a solitary affair, nurtured by a stack of porno magazines in the attic at home. In the presence of female beauty in the flesh—like now—he got totally flustered. Beauty was not for him, and it never would be. No beautiful woman, nor even an ugly one, had ever looked into Jon's face and marvelled at what she saw. He read in the magazines about fat and ugly people, and he suffered with them. But the fel-

42

lowship of the ugly was no fellowship; it was frustrating loneliness, perdition for each and all.

He introduced himself. "I live over there," he said, nodding in the direction from which the rain was coming. "I go hunting around here. . . . Ha-ha. And I work on water pipes. . . ." Then he got to the point. "Do you remember Lisa? That's why I'm talking to you. There was a lot about her in your newspaper. . . ."

The journalist took her time in replying. They were alone. It was dark, and this was not like anything she was accustomed to.

"Lisa?" she mumbled as she jangled her car keys. "No, I don't think so. Besides, I don't have much time. Couldn't we talk about this some other time?"

"She went to Copenhagen to become a ballet dancer. That was in your paper too."

"Yes, that rings a bell. She was from the north side of the island, wasn't she?"

"Yes."

"Daughter of the guy that owns the fish works, if I remember correctly?"

"Right. My age. With long, dark hair, about to here." He pointed to her collar. They were no longer under a roof but out in the rain— she under the umbrella, he far enough away so as not to appear pushy. She made a gesture to indicate that he could join her under the umbrella, but it was not convincing so he stayed where he was.

"She disappeared," he said.

"Disappeared? What do you mean by that? That she didn't come back? Okay. And what do you want me to do about it?"

Not so much. He just wanted to read what they had written about her. There presumably were some archives. He wanted to look at the pictures of her that her father and her sisters had sent in.

She held the umbrella over his head and he took care not to breathe in her face. People don't like to have someone breathe in their face, especially when they have just been obliged against their will to do someone a favor.

43

"There shouldn't be any problem with that. When would you like to do it?"

She took another look at her watch and made a restless movement. He hurried out into the rain again.

"No, no," she said crossly. "Don't do that!"

He didn't understand.

"Don't stand out in the rain. Stand here under the umbrella until we are done talking. You make me nervous."

"Okay."

"You're soaking wet, and you look like a . . . Good lord, what am I saying?"

"It doesn't matter."

"Yes, yes, of course I remember Lisa," she said quickly. "But it was one of the first stories I covered. It must have been over two years ago. The Oslo newspapers followed the story of her disappearance too, didn't they?"

"Yes."

"And she never came back?"

"No."

"Strange."

Jon held the umbrella while she unlocked the car door and got in, then handed it to her through the window. "Shall we say sometime next week, then?"

He nodded and she looked at him.

"Are you just going to stand here?"

Maybe she was thinking of offering him a ride, but he knew how to help people out of embarrassing situations of that sort.

"No, thanks," he said, anticipating the offer. "I'm going north."

The motor was running but still she lingered for a few seconds.

"My name is Marit," she said, offering him her hand. "I don't know if I can help you, but ask for Marit when you come . . . *if* you come. Okay?"

"Okay."

"And excuse me."

44

"For what?"

"Oh, Good lord. Forget it."

She raised the window and drove off. Jon waited until the lights disappeared around the corner, then began walking slowly in the same direction.

He thought of Lisa's eyes, which had not left him for a minute since they had showed up again that day outside the administration building; that strange squint of hers, like two mirrors that weren't adjusted quite correctly. It wasn't just Jon whose composure was shaken by them. Almost everybody was amazed that an oddball like Lisa could look so beautiful.

He was so preoccupied that he didn't notice the car until he was right beside it—a new Subaru parked on a side road where you could look out over the marshland. It was Hans's car. He walked over to it, pressed his face against the windshield and looked in— but there was nothing to see. Nor could he hear any sound from the woods nearby except the continuously pounding rain. Suddenly the reflection of two headlights appeared on the wet glass; they were approaching from the east, on the road from the inner side of the island. Acting on impulse, he returned to the roadway and positioned himself so that he would be seen. It was the journalist coming back. She saw him, slammed on the brakes and stepped out of the car.

"What are you doing here?" she asked with a hint of irritation. "I thought you said you were going north?"

"I'm standing here and looking at that car," he answered matter-of-factly. "It belongs to a teacher."

She looked at the car.

"Well, so what? Has something happened?"

Through the trees they could glimpse a faint light.

"There's a farm over there," he said. "It isn't farmed any more. The man works in the city and his wife lives there alone. On the other side of the field there's another farm. Do you see it? One of his former pupils lives there."

45

He shrugged his shoulders. "Maybe he isn't at either place."

"I don't understand. Are you out spying on him?"

"Well . . . he sees my sister. I'm doing it for her."

She started to laugh, but her eyes betrayed more concern than amusement. She was as wet as he was now and her makeup had started to run. Her hair, which earlier in the evening had stood up smartly, lay flat against her scalp and looked like broken spikes.

"Can I drive you home?" she asked impatiently. "Or do you want to stay here?"

"Sure."

"Get in, then—before we drown."

They drove south for a few hundred meters, then turned off the highway and continued on the carriage road. It was old and poorly maintained. In several places it had been undermined by rushing torrents of water. Originally it led over toward the neighboring island, but nobody had lived there for a long time. During a storm the previous winter the bridge had been destroyed by ice, so now the path just led to the main farmyard and the house beyond it where Jon and Elisabeth lived.

He sat and ran his fingers over her camera and pretended that he didn't hear her complaining about the conditions. "Farther," was all he said when she began to stop in the farmyard. She complied, but reluctantly.

It was pitch dark. There was no horizon, no light of any kind. The road got worse and worse the farther they drove. As they drove down the hill and through the grove, the road became almost impassable. The journalist stopped several times, but it was impossible to turn around and Jon urged her to go on.

When they finally got to Jon's house he explained slowly and in great detail how she should turn around without backing into the grindstone in the dark. When he was finished he remained sitting and looked at her, making no move to get out. She avoided his gaze.

"You're scared," he said, and he felt a certain pleasure as she bit her lower lip. This was *his* world, the only spot on the face of the earth where *he* was in control.

"I should never have done this," she sighed.

"No," said Jon. "You shouldn't."

They listened to the rain that continued to pound on the roof of the car. Her polished nails clung tightly to the steering wheel, and she never took her eyes off the windshield wipers' futile struggle with the water.

"Does this mean that I'm a prisoner?"

That was presumably an attempt at humor, but Jon did not answer. It was not often that he had an opportunity to use his lordly smile, which he had practiced for such a long time in front of the mirror. Against Elisabeth, and against anyone else who knew him, it was useless; it required a stranger. He was going to enjoy it for just a little longer.

"I can't handle this," she said. "Do something!"

Jon remained silent. "What do you want?" she shouted.

He opened his mouth, closed it again, and sat for a few more seconds. Then he calmly laid the camera in her lap, opened the door, and got out. She lunged across the seat and locked the door behind him. But then she couldn't get the car turned around, and after several unsuccessful attempts she had to roll down the window again and accept directions from Jon. He instructed her step by step. The car lurched forward and stopped. Through the window he saw her lay her head against the steering wheel in mute despair.

"There's nothing to be afraid of," he said.

She regained control, started the motor, and sped away down the bumpy road.

Jon was not an evil person. He had held her life in his hands and had not taken it. He had not even touched her. He didn't want power in order to misuse it. In his dreams, where everything he did had significance, he did good deeds: he gave to those who were in need, he protected people and freed them from their prison cells. Actually, everyone was in prison, behind visible or invisible bars. This evening had ended like a fairy tale.

Elisabeth sat knitting when he came in, alone. He dried his hair with a towel.

"Who were you riding with?" she asked immediately.

"With Hans," he said elatedly. He started the video camera and pointed it toward Elisabeth.

"Don't do that," she said. "You know I don't like it."

He laughed and continued to let the camera roll. "Jon!" she said. "I don't know what I'm supposed to do!"

"Don't do anything," he said. "Just sit still and knit."

"I told you I don't like it!"

He left the camera running and sat down in the rocking chair with the towel around his head.

"With Hans?" she asked skeptically. "Why didn't he come in with you?"

"I have no idea. Wanted to get home to his wife, I think."

"Don't be silly. He would never have driven all the way out here without stopping in."

"I suppose not."

"You're lying, aren't you?"

He rocked slowly back and forth without answering.

"You're still on," he said, nodding toward the camera.

"Who drove you home?" she screamed. "Answer me, you idiot!"

"I told you: Hans."

"And where did you meet him, if I may ask?"

"Down by Grinda."

He had touched a nerve, and he got ready to rescue the camera in case she lost her temper.

"You're disgusting," she said. To mention Grinda was clearly going too far. It could be a confirmation of her worst suspicions about a rival for Hans's affections. "You're a dirty dog, do you know that?"

48

He relished the moment.

"And turn off that damned camera or I'll smash it!"

Ordinarily Jon had no control in situations like this. He just kept on pressing until she broke into tears, smashed something, or left the house. But this time they were interrupted by the sound of a motor. A light swept across the windows, and a car stopped out in the yard.

Jon and Elisabeth looked at each other. Elisabeth gave no indication of what she was thinking. Jon turned off the camera, put it back in the corner and sat down.

They waited, but nobody came to the door. Finally Jon went outside.

"It's Hans," he said when he came back.

"Oh?" she said dryly and indifferently, again full of self-control. "Why doesn't he come in?"

"He wants to know if he can take a shower here."

"Shower?"

Slowly it dawned on her what was going on.

"Yes," said Jon sympathetically. He quickly understood that he had hit the tender nail on the head, and this really was not the way he wanted to see her. "He's drunk as a coot. He needs help."

"I'm not going to help that tomcat," she said softly. "You do it, or else let him sit there."

Jon had no intention of even touching him. He took the video cassette out of the camera and wrote with a pen beside number 5 on the label: "Three minutes with Elisabeth when I told her that Hans drove me home." Adding the date and time, he signed his name and filed it away.

"It wasn't Hans who drove me home," he said. "It was that woman journalist who was at the concert."

He exited the drama and went up to his room. From there he heard Elisabeth drag her lover into the house, heard also her indignant reproaches and his sniveling defense: life had backed him into a corner, this evening was an accident and a onetime occurrence.

Then he heard the sound of water being run into the bathtub, voices that began to sound more conversational. Then whispering, interrupted now and then by snickering and laughter. For a long time it was quiet. Then there were steps on the stairway, muffled laughter, doors opening and closing, and at last the creaking of the bed springs announcing that their reconciliation was complete.

Jon did not sleep that night. He had allowed himself to experience the euphoric feeling of being in control, which he obviously was not. That realization even softened his hatred for Hans. He *knew* that the fellow was nothing but a piece of flotsam adrift on the sea, and that he, too, was just doing the best he could, the bastard.

It stopped raining. When the first rays of the sun peeped through the curtains and struck the poster where Johnny Cash was singing "Joshua gone Barbados," there were again signs of life in the room next door. Footsteps on the stairway and humming in the kitchen. The smell of fresh coffee wafted through the house, and when the car finally started out in the yard he fell asleep.

7

They got a new compressor. But the farmer who owned it insisted that he be hired in order to keep an eye on the equipment, and they no longer needed Jon.

Rimstad came during the morning coffee break and tramped around in his new boots. He looked dejected, said the budget was tight and didn't allow him to hire an extra man. He was sorry about it.

Jon said it didn't matter. He knew that agreements between poor people and benefactors always end like this. Rimstad was not to worry, Jon could go hunting again. No doubt the rabbits would turn white before the snow came this year too, the idiots. Ha-ha. Or he could do nothing at all, as usual.

But he was no longer accustomed to doing nothing. They had had *use* for him during these weeks, and he enjoyed being with the divers. It was as if the three of them were in their own Klondike, welded together by their tough work.

So in the days that followed he spent a lot of time standing around and feeling foolish. He looked at the grindstone with the crank lying in the grass, and at the old leaning fence that needed to be fixed. But it was as if there were no meaning in any of this, for they were going to move. He thought a little, tried to dream. He had always been good at dreaming. There was, for example, no place in the world where he had not been, no conflict that he had not resolved, no person in need whom he had not saved. But this time his dreaming didn't amount to anything. Besides, he had reawakened the remnant of his work ethic. In the middle of the day

51

one ought to *do* something—go out in the field and dig with a spade, take down an electric fence in preparation for winter, put out nets to get a little food in the house, *something*.

Only very slowly, much more slowly than the last time he had had work, was Jon able to resume his futile indifference. But he managed it. And if he didn't exactly forget the divers and the aqueduct, at least he missed them less and less.

Then one day Georg suddenly turned up again, arriving via one of the paths through the marsh. Jon put down the ax he was sharpening—he had finally decided to chop a little wood—and fled into the house so as not to be seen. But the diver followed him, so Jon had to go up to his room. A few minutes later Elisabeth came.

"One of the divers is here," she said.

"I know," he said indifferently as he continued to poke around in a drawer.

"He's waiting."

"Okay."

"He's sitting down in the kitchen."

"Understand."

Why couldn't that SOB stay away, now that he had forgotten him?

"I'm sorry about what happened," he said when Jon came down. Elisabeth had cooked coffee and there was a plate of cookies on the table. Store-bought cookies, the kind Jon usually picked up when he got tired of nagging her to bake. He ignored the diver's apology and asked him what he wanted.

"Can you help me today? It takes four men to open the valves. And besides, the farmer can't climb."

"Climb?"

"Yes. We have to go up to the reservoir in the mountain."

Jon slurped noisily before he answered.

"No," he said.

The diver looked surprised. He obviously thought of Jon as a resource that one could make use of as needed.

52

"What do you mean by that?"

"Just what I said: *no.*"

"Well, is that all you have to say?"

That was all he had to say. He was done with both the aqueduct and the divers. He couldn't care less about the new water. It had nothing to do with life. It was superfluous, ludicrous.

"Are you doing something else?"

"No."

"Well, then, do you want more money?"

"No."

Georg raised his voice. "Couldn't you give us just a few hours this afternoon, then? We *need* one more man, and nobody else will do it."

Jon was adamant, but offered no explanation.

Georg stood up, bewildered. Elisabeth said nothing, merely looked reprovingly at her brother. She had failed him again the previous night and lacked standing to upbraid him in front of others.

The diver threw his arms in the air in a gesture of frustration.

"All right, then," he said.

He said "All right, then" once more, looked imploringly at Jon and Elisabeth, and left without having accomplished anything.

Jon followed him out to the steps.

"Don't go that way," he shouted when the diver was about a hundred meters away. "You might sink in the mud."

The man stopped, looked down at the path he had been walking on, and went back a few steps.

"What do you mean? It's the same path I came on, isn't it?"

Jon didn't answer right away. Then all he said was, "Okay." Softly.

He sat down carefully on the steps, like a spectator in an arena where any moment there might be a life-and-death struggle. His well-polished gun lay over his knees, with tiny dewdrops glistening on the dull oiled metal. The sky above was clear, and there was no wind, but the mountains to the south were enveloped in fog. To

53

those who knew the area it was obvious that a storm was brewing. It might break out in twenty minutes, in five hours, or tomorrow evening.

Georg shook his head resignedly, left the path through the marsh and began walking down the main road. Jon called out to him again: "Why are you going that way?"

"What?"

"Why are you going that way when you came the other way?"

Georg was about out of patience. "What the hell are you up to?" he asked angrily. "Are you trying to make a fool out of me, or what?"

Jon stood up, raised the gun into position, pressed the stock against his cheek, and saw the diver's pale face fill the whole circle behind the cross-hairs for two, three short seconds. Then he pulled the trigger.

"Yes," he said.

Georg stood stiffly in the gray light, legs apart, arms at his side.

The metallic click awakened two crows on the fence, who cawed shrilly as they flew away. Some birch leaves clung to Georg's muddy boots.

Jon lowered the gun and went into the house, slamming the door behind him.

But the idleness was precarious. His empty days had been knocked askew all over again. What did the divers really want from him? He grew restless. And the morning the storm began he dressed in his best clothes in preparation for a trip to the city to talk with the journalist.

Black velvet pants and brown leather jacket—not exactly the latest style, but fairly straight up and down, with a couple of buttons near the top that really shouldn't be there. He ripped one of them off, but that didn't improve it much. Light blue shirt, freshly ironed. Most of his trips to the city were difficult. He had only to remember one or two of his less fortunate appearances and he could feel the blush of shame creep over his skin like a grass fire. He remembered one time when he had had the misfortune of knocking over a table in a cafe. *Everybody* was looking at him. His clothes had never been in worse disarray than in that place in the middle of the forenoon; his hair was mussed, his back was bent, and he felt uglier than ever.

He stood by the window to motivate himself, stared gloomily down the road where strong gusts of wind were pounding the gravel. At least there wouldn't be many people out on the streets.

"You're not bad looking when you get dressed up," Elisabeth said, looking at him from the back.

He shuddered.

"I'm ugly," he said. "Ugly as hell!"

"Good Lord, what are you saying?" she cried, looking frightened.

"Shut up or I'll throttle you!"

He opened the billfold that his father had made out of soft pigskin. Apart from the house, the boathouse, and a few acres of worthless land, his father's most personal effects constituted Jon's most cherished mementos.

"I don't understand you," said Elisabeth. "You've become so impossible."

"I've always been that way. Can you lend me a couple hundred crowns?"

"Of course. But then we should be able to talk to each other. Don't you think it would be best if you started taking your medicine again?"

"No."

"But you're never calm. And what kind of thoughts are raging around in your head?" She handed him the money. "Those medications are for your own good."

"You told me I was doping myself when I used to take them. 'Chemicals are harmful,' you said. I got a puffy face and slept all day. Don't you remember?"

He left without waiting for an answer.

In the cellar he found an old raincoat that he could take off at the wharf and store under some crates until he came back. Once aboard the hydrofoil he bought fifty one-crown coins at the ticket window, then spent the time on the trip playing the slot machines in the lounge.

As they neared the promontory on the south side of the island, the sea became rough. The pontoons smashed against the surging waves like giant pistons, and the captain had to reduce his speed. The sea grew more calm as they passed between some small islands and the mainland, but on the last leg of the trip over the fjord it was as rough as it had been earlier. By the time they docked at the wharf in the city the mountains on the island were totally hidden by clouds. The fishing fleet was heading for port. In a short time most of the coastal traffic would cease and airplanes would no longer be able to land. A tattered pennant on the roof of the maritime building made a sound like a rifle as it whipped in the wind. The first storm of autumn hung oppressively over the entire region.

Protected by a row of storage sheds, Jon was able to make his way toward the center of the city. He walked through the old coal storehouse and out onto the deserted Main Street. The newspaper office was on one of the side streets, and he was met by a young man in a gray suit who looked embarrassed when Jon shook the water off his jacket. He said that Marit was not in—she was covering a soccer match in a neighboring community—but Jon understood from the strained look he gave to an older colleague nearby that this was just a fib.

"Okay," he said amiably. "I'll come back, then."

"It could be awhile."

"That doesn't matter."

"Possibly several hours."

"Doesn't matter."

Jon recognized this facial expression. It was that of an honest man who was trying to be kind by telling a lie. But Jon had been preyed upon all his life. He was a jackrabbit and a victim and he knew how to play the game. He could have said something about the fact that he understood that Marit didn't want to see him, but that would have been embarrassing for the man who was trying to be so kind. So instead he went out and walked across the street. A new office building was under construction there, and a scaffolding had been attached to the front of the edifice. Jon climbed up a couple of levels, and sure enough, he saw Marit hunched over a desk one floor above the office that he had just left.

He went back to the young man with whom he had spoken earlier. It took a little while before he understood what Jon was saying. "I told you she's not here! She's out on a story! Do you want it in writing?"

Humiliated, he slunk off to a sitting area just inside the door and began to plan how he would ask for her forgiveness—both for the episode in the darkness on the island and for the difficulties he had created here.

Suddenly a car pulled up by the sidewalk outside the office, and there she was. Dressed in gray from head to toe. Wide, billowing sleeves that looked like sea-gull wings; tall, black leather boots; a new hairdo—and looking, if possible, even more beautiful than she did the last time he had seen her.

"What's wrong with you?" she asked anxiously, shaking him. Jon had lost consciousness for a moment.

"Nothing," he stammered.

"You look so strange. Are you feeling faint?"

He thought about the woman he had seen behind the desk up on the second floor, and about the young man whose attitude he had so thoroughly misunderstood. The memory of Georg's face blended into these thoughts, as did also the work on the aqueduct and the figure he had seen in the water under the divers' boat a long time ago.

"I was mistaken," he said with a smile.

Her nimble fingers quickly removed her gloves and unsnapped the gray raincoat with dark water-spots on its shoulders. She tossed her head to one side in a way that he had seen her do before, and that presumably was a holdover from a time when she had longer hair. Jon liked long hair. He thought she looked like Lisa.

"Let's go and look in the file," she said authoritatively, taking him by the arm. She was accustomed to dealing with these simple folk from the coastal area who had an inborn fear of media and the public.

She guided him through a massive door and down a small corridor with tall cabinets on each side. They pulled out drawers and looked through row after row of envelopes.

They found newspaper clippings with pictures of Lisa that the family had supplied when she disappeared and a search was undertaken. That was a little over two years ago. These clippings were now gray and faded and made her look distant and ordinary, one among many in the huge collection of miscellaneous faces. Her father, old man Sakkariassen, was there too, standing on the wharf near his place of business, in tight-fitting coveralls that followed the contour of his huge belly. He had asked the public for help in locating his daughter—in Copenhagen, on the island, or someplace in between. They had combed the area for her, but the search was almost pro forma, for most people took it for granted that she was in Copenhagen.

For Jon the whole episode was a blur. He had been sick at the time, numb with fever. And it was no big deal, even though all the clippings may have made it look as if it were. Hundreds of people disappeared every year, and most of them eventually turned up again. Of those that didn't turn up, only a few cases were accorded criminal status; the rest were regarded as tragedies, people whom one almost expected to disappear: alcoholics, suicides, deranged and mentally retarded people. They quickly disappeared from the newspapers and slipped silently into the world of oblivion. They became taboo, their names being mentioned thereafter only because of a slip of the tongue or sheer tactlessness.

The young people on the island had put up a big poster that said, "Come back, Lisa. We love you all the same."

This "all the same" was an expression of the remorse of those who had mistreated and tormented her. With public confessions of this type they got rid of their guilt.

"That's not her," he mumbled regarding the idiotic descriptions of all of Lisa's "good sides."

"What do you mean, 'that's not her'?"

He could have answered that, for example, they had failed to note her fine eyes, but he didn't like the journalist's smile. She kept expecting him to be odd or pathetic, in any case something completely different from the menacing and self-confident character she must remember from the island—which is the way he liked to be.

"I'm the one who has gathered the clippings from the other newspapers," she said. "There was something special about the story, a young woman who leaves these parts to go to Copenhagen to become a ballet dancer. That's pretty extraordinary, don't you think?"

"Hmm."

"And now she's missing again, isn't that right?"

"I don't know . . . No, she's working some other place."

"Are you in love with her?"

"No."

"There's certainly nothing wrong with that. Everybody falls in love now and then."

Being in love was not the right word. That was the illness afflicting Elisabeth, the throbbing erosion that lay and gnawed at the community when the darkness of night settled over the island. It had nothing to do with him and Lisa.

He put the clippings back and placed the envelope where it belonged in the file.

"Will you try to find her?"

No, he didn't know. That wasn't why he had come. Just now he was mainly concerned about getting out of this place. There were no more disturbing things to discover here than there had been in the ordinary work day of the divers.

"I could help you try to trace her. Something might come out of it anyway."

"Of what?"

"The story—if you don't mind? We don't dig around in people's private lives without their permission."

He didn't take the opportunity to say that she should mind her own business. All he said was, "Maybe."

She had taken his arm again and they were on their way out.

"So her family didn't like it that she wanted to become a dancer?"

"No. Nobody else did either."

"But could she dance?"

He thought about it. Yes, Lisa could dance, better than some, but perhaps not in the way that most other people thought was good. And that was probably also part of the story of her first stay in Copenhagen. Jon had a feeling that when she came back she looked inwardly like he did now: dark. That, in any case, was the first time he had sensed some changes in her.

He walked aimlessly through the empty streets as he waited for the next boat, avoiding the cafes and waiting rooms and hoping that the storm would wipe out the memory of the meaningless visit to the newspaper office. As if that file could contain anything of interest. But then he had been sick at the time, and remembered nothing of what had happened.

Outside the hotel he caught sight of a familiar figure—Hans—who walked out of the lobby and disappeared in between the warehouses by the harbor. He headed the same way and caught up with him down by the wharf, where the teacher was standing in the shelter of a shed and reading a sign.

"The hydrofoil has been cancelled," he said and swore as Jon came up beside him. "Are you on your way home?"

"Hmm."

"It doesn't look promising. So you've been to the city, Jon?"

Yes, he had.

"You know, it's just amazing, the things that determine what happens to you in this life. The weather gets bad, and all of a sudden everything gets turned upside-down."

And as the teacher philosophized irritably about the bad weather, Jon thought about the fact that from his sister's perspective that was how a handsome man looked. A moustache that is in just the right place, a high, clean-cut forehead with a slight depression at each temple, philosophical-looking blue eyes, and a nose so centrally located that it was almost an exaggeration. Nobody had ever laughed at this person, no matter how many dumb things he might have done. He had a free ticket to life, no matter what. Jon thought to himself that if he were ever to kill anyone, this is the kind of person it would have to be.

"Why don't you get a divorce," he suddenly blurted out, "and marry Elisabeth?"

The teacher looked as if he were going to fall into the sea.

"What kind of silly talk is that? She hasn't put you up to that nonsense, has she?"

"No, I just said it on my own."

"Yes, of course. You have a bit of an imagination, my boy. That's something I've learned about you."

"It's a good thing you aren't my teacher any more. Ha-ha."

"Yes, thank heaven. But now you want me for a brother-in-law?"

"No. But then she wouldn't go away. I don't want to go away."

Hans gave him a long, sad look. The storm had filled the entire space between the island and the mainland, and the sea gushed like a pulsating waterfall through the opening in the breakwater. On the wharf a forklift picked up a pallet loaded with milk cartons and moved it over to a place near the ferry landing.

"Yes, yes, I understand what you're saying," mumbled the teacher. "After all, who wants to leave everything he has. I hope you realize that that applies to me too."

"No."

"Okay. But be thankful."

"Thankful for what? She wants you, doesn't she?"

"As if she wouldn't have been going away if she got me—or *didn't* get me, as far as that goes."

That sounded like pure nonsense to Jon. He had a vacant expression, and Hans explained patiently that going away had nothing to do with the matter. "That's just a pretext, something she uses to . . . uh . . . put pressure on me."

"Do you think she won't leave after all?"

"I don't know."

"Well, what do you think then?"

Hans looked resignedly across the wharf where the forklift was returning from the ferry dock.

"It looks like the ferry is about to leave," he said. "You could take *it*."

He smiled briefly. "Elisabeth doesn't like living on the island any more," he said. "She wants to leave. And she wants me to go along. Whether we get married or not has nothing to do with that decision. It might even be that . . ." He left the sentence hanging.

" . . . that it is best if you *don't* get married?" Jon asked impatiently and hopefully. But that couldn't be what the teacher thought, for now he looked even more resigned. He began to walk away.

"Do yourself a favor," he said over his shoulder. "Stop thinking. You'll never understand this anyway."

Jon wasn't finished.

"Where are you going?" he shouted. "Aren't you taking the ferry?"

"I've been to the hospital to visit a boy who broke his arm in the schoolyard. Since his parents won't be coming now, I can just as well stay here. Say hello to Elisabeth."

Jon made his way uncertainly through the storm, following the forklift over to the ferry dock and clambering aboard. There was still no visible, palpable force that was tearing down his home, just the same usual stealthy erosion. It ate away at the soil around the roots of the plants, pelted the petals with wet sand and capricious winds. It went on night and day, whether he sat still or did something. A clock.

There was a slot machine on the ferry, too. Jon won 52 crowns during the trip home, so his pockets were bulging as he walked off the ferry and into the waiting bus. He had never won that much before. He took it as a good sign.

8

The storm raged for over three days, which was longer than usual. Then it let up as quickly as it had begun, and that morning Jon left home just as it was beginning to get light and headed southward through the marshes on the same path he had formerly taken on his way to work.

At Long Lake the waves had etched a deep trench into the shoreline. Chunks of sod thrown up by the pounding surf lay all around, a yellow-white scum still clung to the heather, and the stack of pipes that Jon had sawed was heaped up in wild disarray like a logjam. It was cold and clear, and the glow of a golden sun was just over the horizon. The three men were sitting around the bonfire.

Once again it was Georg who first caught sight of him, and he was just as negative as he had been the first time.

"What do you want here?" he shouted.

But Jon knew him now. He knew that it was mainly the bad weather and not *him* that was eating at the diver's nerves. He calmly opened the sack and began to put on his oilskin coveralls.

"We've lost several days because of you," said Georg. But even as he said it he handed him a cup of coffee.

"Well, at least you weren't wiped out."

No, they weren't. The boat had been secured way up in the woods, and they had tied down the crew shed so it wouldn't blow over.

They had also had to fill the new water pipe and sink it, so most of the forenoon had been taken up with raising it again and getting the end properly placed in the concrete reservoir that had been created at the edge of the lake. They fastened it to the gridwork that the construction workers had laid down during the summer, and in the afternoon Georg and Jon headed over to the other side.

They went ashore in the cove where the pipes, enclosed in insulated wooden cases bolted to solid rock, came down from the reservoir at the top of the mountain. They began climbing upward. When they had climbed a couple hundred meters or so, Georg stopped and turned around. He had been quiet most of the day, but Jon had assumed that it was because of the weather and the delay in the work. Now he realized that the diver had something else on his mind.

"Why did you come back?" he asked in a quiet but menacing tone of voice.

Jon looked at him but said nothing. Wasn't it obvious?

"To make more trouble?"

"No."

They were standing on a narrow ledge, Georg a few steps higher than Jon. A misstep here would mean a fall of a good hundred and fifty meters through thin air. Wispy clouds flitted here and there at this altitude, and the northernmost part of the lake—where their camp was situated—was out of sight. Jon held a pipe wrench in his hand.

"We're nearing the end," Georg said cryptically.

"Oh?"

"And I don't want you to spoil it for me."

That wasn't Jon's intention either. He was here to take part in the conclusion and for no other reason, he could swear to that.

"You scared me with that rifle, do you know that?"

"It wasn't loaded."

"So I noticed."

65

Then came something Jon hadn't expected. "It was you who made the compressor fall into the marsh too, wasn't it? And we're not going another step until you tell me why."

Jon looked around, up into the clouds, down toward the jagged rocks. He realized that this had been planned. Georg had set a trap to force him to confess.

"I did it because I thought they would dig it up again," he said. "I thought they would dig up the marsh."

"And why should they dig up the marsh?"

"I don't know."

"Don't know?"

"No."

"Do you have any idea what a compressor like that costs?"

"No."

The ensuing silence sounded like a soft murmur in his eardrums. Jon could not even hear their breathing. It was unbearable.

"Are you scared?" Georg asked derisively.

"No. I've got a pipe wrench in my hand."

It was not Georg that scared him but the sense of foreboding as to what all this might imply.

Suddenly Georg broke out in a spasm of idiotic laughter and began instead to look out over the landscape—the sea and the marshland—insofar as it was visible through the gaps in the cloud cover. Finally, without saying a word, he turned around and continued climbing. Jon waited until Georg had advanced ten meters or so, then followed after him.

The reservoir, a crater-like depression in the side of the mountain, lay some five hundred meters above sea level and was fed by innumerable little streams that tumbled down the mountainside. It was only about a hundred meters in diameter, but deep enough to supply thousands of people with water—an emerald-green circle that looked like an artificial eye set in granite.

A flat surface had been moulded at the outlet, and below it was a small enclosure for the valves. They lay on all fours in the morainal drift and tightened the bolts on the flange. Georg wielded the wrench, Jon did the holding.

Georg was in good spirits.

"There's nothing like getting done with a job," he said. "Then everything loosens up."

He said he had been doing this kind of work for over sixteen years. He had been everywhere, not only in Norway but abroad—India, Itaipu . . .

"What's Itaipu?" Jon asked.

"A man-made dam in South America. It's bigger than this whole island. Thousands of people worked on it around the clock. I was just an inexperienced rookie then, with a company that was there to conduct some tests."

He wiped some sweat from his forehead and remarked that he must be starting to get old. It was hard work. Did Jon know, for example, the average life expectancy of divers in the North Sea?

"No."

He talked away as he never had before—about himself and the rootless life divers lived. Jon understood that it had something to do with finishing the job, when everything loosens up, including the mysterious silence that had characterized this man as long as they had known each other. Already it seemed like an eternity since they had worked overtime welding pipes the evening after Rimstad had cussed them out for losing the compressor.

"Finally!" said Georg with exaggerated relief in his voice when they had finished tightening the last bolt. "Now let's open the valves, okay?"

"Hm," said Jon.

"You can do it—since you've got the pipe wrench. Ha-ha. Jon, damn it all, you're the biggest dolt I've ever met."

Jon straddled one of the pipes and placed the wrench over the brass key on the valve. Georg called Paul on the walkie-talkie and

67

got a go-ahead signal. Jon ceremoniously turned the wrench two complete revolutions—and they heard the gentle sound of water running through the pipe.

"Now do the other one."

Jon did the other one. "Two more turns," said Georg, "and two more on the first one. Then wait until the flushing sound stops."

They waited. Paul came on the walkie-talkie from time to time to say that all the connections were holding, and Georg responded with a curt "Good." Twenty minutes passed. Then the sound stopped. Jon could open the valves all the way—full pressure.

Five more minutes passed.

"Yes!" said Paul on the walkie-talkie.

Georg smiled broadly. He pounded his knuckles against one of the pipes and declared proudly that the job was done, the contractors and the locals could take over the responsibility and the digging that remained. He and Paul could go, pack up, leave . . .

On the way down he stopped once again on the ledge above the dizzying precipice, this time as a new and renewed person. Through an opening in the clouds they caught sight of a cluster of fishing boats bathed in sunlight far out in the sea. Georg drew a deep breath, and Jon suddenly perceived his own world through the eyes of the stranger, and it made his back tingle.

"I see that they've started fishing for herring again," said Georg. "Will they get any?"

"Yes," said Jon. "They'll get plenty."

He explained where the best fishing grounds were and how they caught herring. They weren't permitted to use trawling nets any more. And Georg nodded with interest. He'd like to have a keg of herring to take with him when he headed south if Jon thought that was possible.

"Sure, I can arrange it," he said.

Georg smiled and looked thoughtful.

"Tell me, son," he said seriously, "what is your deepest wish?"

"To rescue someone," said Jon, without thinking about the fact that he was revealing his favorite theme—but that wasn't the point of Georg's question. He wanted to talk about his own wish—to extract from Jon a promise not to make more trouble, not to lay any more obstacles in the way for them. Then *he* would promise in return to forget the matter of the compressor. To be sure, the financial loss was the municipality's, but anyway—could they agree on that?

"Sure," said Jon, that would be fine with him.

"Good. Then we'll get out of here already this evening . . ."

"What about the herring? I'll be bringing the herring tomorrow morning!"

There was something fishy about this sudden excursion into the realm of business ethics, and Jon improvised an idea on the spot.

"No, no," said Georg, "that's not necessary. You needn't bother with it."

"It's no bother."

"Sure it is. I can take care of it myself."

"No, you can't. You don't know anyone here. You don't know how things work."

Georg smiled.

"If you say so. I'll pay you, of course. And one thing more while we're at it: if you should happen to feel like telling someone something—a story, for example, about us and the work out here . . . well . . . forget it, okay? Or at least wait until we're gone."

"Why?"

"We've had a few problems along the way. We don't want any more now. We're done. We've been here long enough. Okay?"

"Okay."

"Good. I know you think I'm an SOB. I haven't treated you much better than all the others do, but it wasn't me that fired you. It was Rimstad. I tried to get him to keep you on."

Jon nodded. "Why shouldn't I tell a story?" he asked.

Georg stared disbelievingly at him, confused and trembling with

69

irritation—like the time when Jon had made him uncertain about which road to take through the marshes.

"We had an agreement about it!" he screamed. "Just now!"

Jon smiled calmly.

"Well, didn't we?"

Jon continued smiling.

Georg said, "You're really crazy, aren't you?"

"It was you that said it. So I suppose I am, then."

Georg stared as if he wanted to strip away the many layers of inflamed tissue that concealed Jon's being. He wanted an answer, but there was no answer. Nothing was going to happen. Nothing happened.

They gazed again at the majestic view. Silently. Georg hadn't noticed the melancholy beauty until now. One gets bogged down and doesn't notice it until it is too late, until one is about to leave and the picture has acquired its deeper tones of loss. As bewildering as madness. Jon was on the verge of tears. He felt a surge of desperation as he thought of old Nils with his whole miserable life spread around on those fields out there. It was a long time since they had sat together on the stone by the shore and watched the sea gulls. He would go there again tomorrow, as quickly as possible, before the old man disappeared too, senile and consumed by forgetfulness— but perhaps, nonetheless, the last human remnant of life as it once was on the island, of life as Jon wanted it to be.

Back at the camp, Paul was sporting a necktie outside his blue denim coveralls. A bottle of champagne and glasses had been placed on the top of the tank. For the rest of the day they sat on the tank and drank, looked down at couplings and valves, examined them carefully for droplets of water, and listened for any sound that might indicate a leak. They saw nothing and heard nothing. Everything was as it was supposed to be.

70

9

A hot, dry wind suddenly began blowing over the island, like a
fire in the middle of autumn. The brown grass crunched under his feet as he walked northward toward the fish works to buy
herring. He had a migraine. He thought about the old cat back at
the house, a hunter whom rheumatism had transformed into a piece
of furniture in which the past stirred only now and then in the long
spring evenings. He wondered if the cat couldn't be put to some use,
if it might not have a place in his new plans.

Jon had many plans now. Among other things, he had looked in
on Nils and Marta and had promised to stop back later in the day.
He thought he was going to need the old man, now that the work
with the divers was finished and most everything around him was
disintegrating.

It also felt good to go back to the fish works. It seemed like years
since he had last been there.

Two fishing boats were tied up and unloading their catches
when he arrived. There were herring scales everywhere, glittering
in the sunshine—on the wharf, on shipping containers and cranes,
on people and boats, just like in those glory days of fifteen or twenty
years ago that people were always talking about. Life and movement all over the place. Whitewashed workbenches had been set
up in the salting room, men and women in bloody aprons gutted the
fish and cut them up, salted, flushed out boxes, poured brine, rolled
barrels back and forth across the wet concrete floor.

The herring still created a revolution in the year's otherwise sluggish rhythm. People came out of their houses, left their tractors, abandoned road work and home building to don white aprons and work with herring and salt hour after hour, day after day for one or perhaps two weeks—depending on how long it took the authorities to figure out that they had long since exceeded their quota.

Jon waved to people right and left. He knew them all. He listened with delight to the laughter and boisterous talk, to the sound of running water, humming boat motors, a radio with the day's jarring news. He watched as a fellow drove a forklift around with big salt bins on the front. The squeaking and squealing of the cranes reverberated in the empty boxes, and over the boats and the buildings flew huge flocks of shrieking birds.

He was back. This was how he saw life in his dreams and in his memory.

He went up the stairs to the cooper's shop, where the smell of fresh-cut spruce filled his nostrils. There were new barrels, waxed barrels, old unwaxed barrels brown with salt and rust and blood, fish boxes and piles of nets, floats, kelp, and acrid fish oil. The dark loft was filled with noise, with the sound of the cooper's hammer striking the wooden casks, and with the sea gulls that hovered endlessly around the opening in the far end. Here was his childhood in large doses, the way it ought to be in a complete and secure world.

The old dungaree-clad cooper looked up and flashed a toothless smile.

"I want a quarter-size barrel," Jon said. But after they had greeted each other and said the usual things about the weather and common acquaintances, the old fellow said that he no longer had quarter-size barrels. "Nowadays," he said, "we only have full-size barrels."

But Jon went into an anteroom, threw aside some old ropes, and pulled down a pile of stuff with some quarter-barrel staves that lay hidden way up under the rafters. He knew every nook and cranny in this loft. This was where he had eaten his stolen food, together with Lisa. Here they had shed their baby teeth together and plotted the

72

final retaliation, their revenge against all those—grown-ups and others—who tormented and reproved them. Here they had been free to enjoy their little scrap of youth. Here they had been able to be a little grown-up, too, with no fear of any serious reprisals.

He recognized the swallow nests up under the ridge of the roof, the gray-green, half-rotten hemp nets where he and Lisa used to capture one another, tarred ropes, trawling nets, lines and fish traps in an abandoned rain forest where make-believe figures had once lived in deep silence. Here were stacks of fishnet floats that you could use to tell fortunes, inflatable tubes to keep you afloat, bamboo poles that you could use to fight and defend yourself, empty spaces that could serve as playhouses, whiskey bottles with magic potions and wonder-working mixtures. Here were barrels and corks and fish hooks and sinkers and pieces of canvas and wooden tubs—worn-out, cast-off items of equipment, each with its own unique story. And undergirding it all was the hustle and bustle of the machinery, of herring and work and things of value.

"Here it is," Jon mumbled reverently. "Where is the old man himself?" He meant Sakkariassen, Lisa's father.

"Well, where do you think?" said the cooper. The quarter-size barrel looked like a growing flower between his huge fists. He held the unruly staves between his knees and forced them into a metal band that he tapped carefully into place. "He's not here, as usual."

"Not even now, when the herring are running?"

"Not even now. He took a look at the first boatload, weighed a few herring to check the size. Then he left again. But it doesn't make any difference, everything runs by itself."

He pressed the last metal band into place. "Maybe things will pick up a little when the new water gets here. A fish works with plenty of fresh water is worth a lot, even today."

Jon looked surprised.

"Is he thinking of selling?"

The old man moved his head from side to side in a gesture of uncertainty.

73

"Who knows? There's a lot of talk, but nobody knows anything."
Jon smiled. If anyone knew anything it was the old cooper. He
had lived in Sakkariassen's farmhouse his whole life. He knew all of
the fish works secrets, both financial and human. But he was stingy
with his knowledge. He had to be bribed, or begged, or tricked, and
Jon wasn't really interested.

He kicked some old kittiwake nests out of the opening and gave
three tugs on the elevator rope. It was no heavier now than before.
Lisa was there, too—everywhere, concealed, pretty and dark-eyed.

"Here," said the cooper as he rolled the little barrel over the
floor. "It has to be soaked. Do you have a net out yourself?"

"What? Uh . . . yeah."

"So you won't be buying the herring here?"

"No."

"Then I'll just charge you for the barrel."

Jon shouldn't have come here. It was getting to be more than he
could handle. She came altogether too close.

He took the barrel and walked out on the wharf. There he met
Frank, a second cousin who had just come in from fishing and
wanted him to come along that evening—they could set out some
more nets. And for a moment he considered it. He enjoyed being
out on the water, just so it didn't turn into a job. But there were too
many other things buzzing around in his head. No, he wouldn't go.

He felt as if his whole life had passed before him up there in the
cooper's loft—the part of his life that was worth something, at any
rate. He remembered that Lisa had said once that he had eyes like a
snake—not because he really did, but because she didn't have much
imagination. He remembered berry bushes in the yard, with clusters
of red currants, black currants, and gooseberries. He saw Lisa's small
white hand, that hand with the delicate pattern of blood vessels,
that slipped in among the redolent wet leaves and wrapped itself
around the juicy clusters, each autumn, over and over again. During
the winter season they filleted sole, they dried fish, hanging it up
on the drying rack, they collected fishbones and nailed codfish

74

heads—these things, too, they did over and over again, in a repetitive ritual. Sakkariassen always saw to it that they were *doing* something, when they absolutely had to be together; kept them occupied, so their hands wouldn't find their way to each other and their bodies become uncontrollable. She had some cookies in the pockets of her apron, green ribbons in her hair, her breath reminded him of every poem he could think of, and most of them had to do with heather and flowers and the sea. Her skin was as smooth and soft as the wing of a seagull under his hard fingertips; he could hardly feel her, no matter how hard he squeezed; he had to lick her, suck on her and make her wet. . . .

He left the fish works in a daze. With the barrel under his arm. Haunted by memories and the maniacal warmth of the dry wind. He was still in a daze when he got to Nils's. They went for a short walk, but he became impatient and wanted to get home. He didn't even take time to taste Marta's freshly baked cookies. He tried to concentrate on the cat again, on the hastily concocted plan that just wouldn't hang together. But all he could think of was Lisa Lisa Lisa. . . . The migraine got worse and worse.

The medicine chest in the bathroom was closed, locked with an iron bolt and padlock—and he himself had thrown the key into the sea. He used a hacksaw to get it open and swallowed a few pills— not too many, but enough to last for the time he would be gone.

She was still there, clearly, right behind him, but the impression was fainter when he was under the influence of the medicine. It was enough to get him through it in any case.

75

10

The new water had to be celebrated.

The soccer field was filled with vehicles and people. Wood panels were placed on sawhorses and covered with paper tablecloths on which were placed cases of bottled soft drinks, trays of sandwiches, and a variety of cakes. Umbrellas and tarpaulins were set up to protect everything from the rain. Rimstad was there, soaking wet in his best suit, and the mayor, bareheaded despite the autumn chill. Schoolchildren and teachers stood in formation, class by class, behind a symbolic barrier of soggy red crepe-paper ribbon. Two journalists were there: Marit, her camera tucked under her stylish raincoat, and a man with a microphone and earphones and a tape recorder on his back. A whole community under an endless downpour.

Elisabeth and two of her friends stood shivering in front of the children. Hans huddled under a misshapen umbrella with his deceived wife, his class directly behind him. Georg and Paul lent an air of authenticity to the occasion by wearing their diving outfits. And in the middle of the open area a single copper pipe protruded from the clay, with a shiny brass faucet on the top festooned in a red ribbon. The new water.

Jon stood in the foreground. Well, perhaps not exactly in the foreground, but not too far back either. Not only had he played a small part in completing the water project, but he also had an expensive video camera on his shoulder, well protected under a plastic bag advertising a familiar brand of coffee.

Two fish boxes had been placed in the center as a podium. After the mayor had spoken a few introductory words, Georg got up on the fish boxes while Jon aimed his whirring video camera at his neck. Georg took off his diver's helmet and told the assembled crowd that the project had been a great challenge both psychologically and physically, a pioneering piece of work. He listed the difficulties caused by weather, transportation complexities, and geography. But now, finally, the water was here. The crowd clapped.

He walked awkwardly in the clumsy diver's suit, stopping in front of Jon and his camera.

"Well, Jon," he said good-naturedly as Rimstad mounted the improvised podium in the background, "I must say I prefer having you aim at me with that thing. That's quite a camera."

"Yes," said Jon as he pointed his camera toward Rimstad.

"Where did you get it?"

"Bought it."

"Hm. It must have cost a bundle?"

"Yeah."

"I'll bet it did."

There's no telling what he has on his conscience today, Jon thought as he took mental note of Georg's vacuous friendliness.

Rimstad was bareheaded now too, with a bunch of wet papers in one hand and a soggy cigarette butt in the other. He was husky-voiced and hoarse and long-winded and serious: it was his unpleasant duty, he said, to pour a little wormwood in the champagne. At present, the waterpipes that would some day bind this scattered hodgepodge of people into one community reached only to *here*— he pointed at the pipe sticking out of the ground. Thus far only the school and the community center were hooked up. All the other pipes had yet to be laid, and that part of the job would be very costly. People must not think that the island consisted of just swamps and heath and sand. No, wherever you stick your finger there is hard rock, granite, that has to be bored and blasted and shoveled away. It would take many years and many annual budgets.

77

But this was at least a beginning. They had made a breach in the wall of prejudice and tradition, and sometime in the future every house, every barn, every business would have water—clean and clear and sparkling fresh water from that emerald-green eye in the mountain instead of that brown slime that stood and rotted in the wells. It *was* a day to be remembered.

More applause.

Then it was the mayor's turn. He spoke loudly and shrilly about finances and administration: the state covers 65% of the cost, he shouted, and the municipality had to come up with the remaining 35% by the sweat of its own brow. This drain on local resources had created conditions as bad as those that obtained at the end of the war—if one might be allowed a slight exaggeration. Some household helpers, farm workers, and day laborers had been forced to seek other employment, for there was little money available for new construction here and even less for maintenance of the old ferry landing or building of a new one. The fire truck was worn out and the idea of a new radio installation at the old people's home would have to remain a pipe dream for some time to come. But everyone needs water, and if there was ever to be any new activity here, one thing was sure: it would require water. Water was the life-giving blood that would bring the island new nourishment and new hope. *Venu vici viri!*

Then, with all eyes upon him, he picked up a pair of scissors, looked up furtively at the leaden sky, and cut the red ribbon on the copper pipe so that clear water could cascade down onto the muddy gravel.

Applause and cheers. Jon's camera whirred, Marit's camera flashed, her colleague held the microphone high in the air. The principal gave a signal, and the school band struck up a march. Then the children sang a song, and the plastic coverings were removed from the tables.

Marit left her colleague with the microphone and walked over toward Georg and Jon. She gave an embarrassed smile as Jon filmed her face.

"Don't be afraid," he said reassuringly. "Everybody looks stupid the first time."

"I hear that you deserve some of the credit for the achievement being celebrated here today," she said cheerfully.

"Aw, not..."

"That's right," said Georg. "He played a role in the most important part of the job. Yessir, if it hadn't been for Jon this celebration would certainly have been delayed for several more days."

Jon responded as he usually did when somebody tried to compliment him.

"I ruined your compressor," he said.

"What?" said Marit.

"I ruined his compressor."

She didn't understand.

"Perhaps I could take a picture of you—you and..."

"Fine, go ahead," said Jon.

He and Georg stood stiffly side by side. The diver obviously didn't like it that Jon had mentioned the compressor, but he didn't say anything.

There were coffee and pastries that had been baked in the school kitchen by the older pupils. They picked up a generous supply, especially Jon, and carried on a vapid conversation about the video camera as they ate. Hans joined them with his youngest son on his shoulders, and he, too, commended Jon for his contribution to the project. Shortly thereafter the radio reporter also appeared and directed his attention to Hans.

"You're on the municipal council, aren't you?" he asked.

"Yes."

79

"I'm especially interested in the financial aspects of the project," he said, holding the microphone between them. "It's a pretty costly undertaking?"

"That it is," Hans said with a smile.

"And it really is the case that this water project will make it necessary to postpone virtually all other municipal projects for the next several years?"

"Uh, yes. I think maybe we haven't been fully cognizant of all the consequences."

"But surely it has all been calculated?"

"The costs, yes. It's the income side that has fallen short. Our tax receipts are low."

"That's true of every municipality that is dependent on fishing and agriculture for its economic well-being. For that matter, as I understand it, the tax receipts haven't been any lower than anticipated, have they? Furthermore, surely a new ferry landing must be more important than water? Especially when you could have had ten ferry landings for the cost of a single water subsystem."

"We don't need *ten* ferry landings," Hans said crossly, "and I'd like to know where you got those numbers."

The reporter told him where he had gotten his numbers, and it sounded impressive.

Jon didn't pay any attention to politics and finances, but it interested him that Hans got more and more agitated as the conversation proceeded.

"Compared with the new school on the mainland side . . ."

Hans cut him off: "Yet another misappropriation, in your opinion? Tell me, is this an interview?"

"Sure, why not. Five million crowns in construction costs, and four teacher positions—for *eight* pupils?"

"There are more than eight."

"Eight. For the next seven years there will be eight—and five of them are the teachers' own children."

Hans rolled his eyes skyward and backed away. Jon thought it was too bad the reporter didn't have a video camera, so he turned his on—to Hans's obvious displeasure. But Hans pulled himself together and told the reporter about the region's political significance and about the cost of a school bus. Besides, he thought they were here to celebrate the successful conclusion of a memorable achievement for coastal communities, namely, the assertion of the same right to clean water as the rest of the country. Why didn't the reporter go instead to the state and reproach it for its irresponsibility?

"At the moment I am interested in how the *municipality* manages the resources available to it," he answered.

"As if we had any choice."

"You have had a choice."

Hans turned and walked away. When he was beyond the range of the microphone he said, "Maybe 65/35 is a tempting number."

Jon didn't get this comment on the videotape either.

"He thinks the water is poisoned," laughed the diver. "God, I'm glad I'm finished here."

"Poisoned?"

"Yup, you'll soon see that the whole island will perish from water poisoning. Ha ha. And hey, thanks for the herring. I've already sent it south." He turned to Marit: "Jon picked up a barrel of herring for me."

She smiled. And while Georg went to get some more coffee and sweet rolls and Jon was putting the camera away, she used the opportunity to whisper secretively, "Did you get my letter?"

He looked surprised. "Letter?"

"Yes, I sent it last week. Apparently nobody knows where Lisa is. The police haven't heard anything. The family says she is visiting relatives, but I haven't been able to get in touch with her."

Jon realized with consternation that it presumably was he who had initiated this curiosity.

"Maybe we should try to speak with her father," she suggested, scanning the crowd.

"He's not here," said Jon. "He stays home, never goes out."

81

"Is he sick?"

"Uh, yeah."

Georg came back with a plate of sandwiches and an extra cup of coffee which he handed to Marit. He was well dressed under his diver's outfit, ready to travel. He had shaved off his beard, and the skin on that part of his face was white. Suddenly one of the children knocked over the container of spiked currant punch, and people scurried to avoid the shower of red liquid. Jon caught the eye of the radio reporter, who was now interviewing Rimstad, and in the background spied Elisabeth, who was just leaving with her girl friends. He left Georg and Marit and caught up with her.

"Did you take the letter that was addressed to me?" he asked when they had walked a short distance.

"Why do you bother me with that now?" she asked sullenly. "Can't you see that I'm depressed?"

Jon had not noticed it, but he understood that it no doubt had something to do with Hans.

"Yes, he was there with his whole family," he said sympathetically. "The wife and the kids. *Four* kids. That sure is too many."

Elisabeth laughed.

"You are much prettier," he continued. "That's nothing to feel sorry about. Did you take the letter that was addressed to me?"

She had been holding his arm. Now she dropped it again.

"No, I haven't *taken* it," she said. "I don't ever take a thing from you. It was in the mailbox, and I put it in the basket on the refrigerator, as I always do. It's still there, unless you have taken it yourself."

Jon had looked in the basket on the refrigerator—as recently as this morning. There was no letter there, but he understood that it would appear there in the course of the afternoon.

"Okay," he said. "And have any letters come previously—from Copenhagen, for example?"

"From Copenhagen? Are you expecting a letter from *Copenhagen?*"

"No, but one could come anyway."

"Not that I know of."

"You're absolutely sure?"

"Of course I'm sure! What's going on here? Don't you trust me any more?"

Jon didn't answer. He couldn't trust anybody. He was a sick man who lived in a sheltered world, among people who said they desired his best. Under such circumstances one had to take certain precautions.

He switched over to the subject of moving again. It had been on the back burner for several weeks. Jon thought it was an appropriate time to talk about the future, since he obviously had not been told the truth about the letters. He remembered that their father had once said that nobody could escape from this island. You took it with you wherever you went, like tracks in the clay. But Elisabeth just sighed when he mentioned it, and took his arm again.

"It's not a matter of escaping," she said. "It's a matter of having a realistic view of things. Nothing *happens* here any more. Nobody builds anything, nobody moves here. Pretty soon nobody will be left here except old people and those who aren't able to find anything else to do. Papa couldn't stand to see that happen either. *He* escaped."

"With clay on his boots." Jon laughed.

"You're terribly funny today," she said.

Jon turned serious again. He said flatly that he didn't think she had a realistic view of things. She was a whiner. New houses *were* being built. There *were* able people in the community. There were *not* fewer people here than in the past—and besides, why didn't she herself find something new to occupy her time?

"I'm a *teacher*," she said dryly.

"He won't go with you," said Jon.

"Who?"

"Hans."

"Don't you think I know that?"

"No."

She took a deep breath. "There are twelve pupils in my class," she said, stressing each word. "Twelve! And there are fourteen in Marianne's. Next year there will be ten in mine and eleven in hers. Do you know what that means?"

"No."

"It means that our classes will be combined. That I will lose my job. It's as simple as that. There is nothing else to discuss."

They were past the curve with the willow trees where Jon had seen Hans's car one night. He was about to say that the broader issue of what was going to happen to them remained to be discussed when he was interrupted by a loud shout. Far off in a field on the right of the road stood a farmer in an oilskin jacket, frantically waving his arms. Jon tried to hide behind his sister.

"Too late," she laughed maliciously. "He saw you."

It was Karl, who cupped his hands around his mouth and shouted again.

"See you later," said Elisabeth as she hurried on.

Jon made his way reluctantly across the ditch and through the barbed-wire fence. There was deep, muddy water in the furrows—so deep that with each step his boots sank in up to the ankles. Karl had worked this piece of land just as his father had done—and his grandfather, and his great-grandfather—and he had the same last name as everyone else who lived in this area. This little farm, like all the other farms hereabouts, had once belonged to a single owner, and the people who lived on the several farms had been sharecroppers. When the estate was divided up, the sharecroppers were all allowed to take the name of the former owner. Karl had a son who was Elisabeth's age, but he became a machinist and built a house a good distance away. He returned only now and then on vacation with his wife and children and sent Christmas cards stating that everything was going fine. But the truth is, said Karl, that he really wishes he were back home, it's that damned city woman he's married to that keeps him away. And Jon, for his part, agreed with him in this, because he didn't like either Karl's daughter-in-law or his grandchildren, who were noisy and cocky and who asked direct questions—such as, Why does one of your eyelids hang down? or, Why are your hands so dirty?

This farm was his second home. The kitchen smelled of cod livers, waffle batter, sour milk, earth, and barn, and when they drank together Karl told stories that had lain buried in his imagination for so long that they had grown overripe and sentimental. Twenty-five years had passed since he had come ashore from his fishing boat and decided that he, too, would become a farmer, just like his father. One day a worldly wise gigolo who roamed the seven seas—Lofoten, Finnmark, even Rockall and Greenland—the next an earthbound slave, surrounded by sheep fences and hostile neighbors.

"If only I had a fraction of the money that has run through these fingers in years past," he sometimes cried when he was drunk. "But I wasn't able to hang on to it. I wasn't able to hang on to it. You have no idea, Jon, for you're just a kid—no idea what I've gone through."

"What happened?" Jon used to ask. "Who took it—the money, I mean?"

"Ohhhhh!"

And in this moan lay a sea of trials and tribulations—life itself, with powers at play that make people commit the most improbable stupidities.

But Jon didn't really enjoy Karl's company very much. There was something wrong with him. He had spent forty thousand crowns on a shiny new roof for an old wreck of a shed. He painted half of one wall of the house and left the rest unpainted. He wrote long letters to the Fund for the Preservation of Nature complaining that the eagles had eaten his sheep, when in fact they had simply wandered off to the mountains because he didn't bother to keep an eye on them. He had a tractor that had to stand on a downhill slope in order to start, and a car that was too nice to ever take out of the garage. Karl's behavior may have been neither better nor worse than that of anyone else in their common struggle to earn their daily bread, but Karl really *believed* that the costly roof was well suited to his broken-down wreck of a shed, that the house looked good with a few strips of green paint here and there, and it made Jon sick to his stomach, perhaps because it reminded him of the darkest side of his own personality. Now Karl was digging potatoes in the driving rain, over a *month* later than everybody else, ostensibly because they grew so tremendously in October.

"Yes, yes," he said as Jon walked up to him. "Well, so fall came again this year too."

Jon nodded and said, "Yeah, it sure did." He looked at the stacks of full and half full wooden buckets, at the potatoes that shone round and wet against the soil.

"Well, what do you say, Jon, are you coming along again this year?"

"Oh, probably," said Jon.

"Yah, I'm not much good in the mountains any more myself, especially not alone."

"No."

"Look here." He bit off a chunk of potato and spit it out. Inside, it was as yellow as an egg yolk. "Strange to find something so fine inside all that crud, ain't it?"

"Yeah."

Silence.

"Penny for your thoughts, Jon."

Jon cleared his throat. "I was wondering if maybe I shouldn't get paid," he said, putting his hands behind his back so as not to appear too offensive.

"Paid? You already get disability pay!"

He had to admit that he did.

"And you've never taken pay before!"

"No."

"Well, what has happened to make things different this time?"

"Ohhh, I dunno. I just thought maybe you'd pay me."

The farmer stared disbelievingly. He threw the potato against the wall of the silo, smashing it to smithereens.

"Nobody takes pay for rounding up the sheep in the mountains," he said testily. "You know that!"

Yes, Jon had to agree that his suggestion sounded silly, but . . .

"And nobody pays *for* it either—do they, now?"

"No."

"Not me, that's for sure."

"No."

"So, where are we?"

"I guess there won't be any pay."

Jon had been looking at the ground most of the time during the conversation. Now he looked out over the fields. "Everything goes 'round and 'round," he mumbled. He felt queasy, presumably as a result of the medicine he had taken.

"What did you say?"

"Everything goes 'round and 'round. I was along last year, I was along the year before that, I've always gone along. I'll be along this year too."

Karl nodded gravely at all this philosophy.

"Yes, yes," he said somberly. "Let's shake on it, then, okay?"

But how would this matter look next year? Jon shuddered. Did he like doing the same thing over and over again? Some of it, yes. Would he like the city? He shuddered again, loosened his boots and prepared to leave. But Karl wasn't finished yet. The discordant conversation had to be rounded off with something a little more pleasant.

"Were you over filming the water celebration?" he asked, nodding toward the camera.

"Yeah."

"Was there anything to shoot, then?"

"Yeah, everybody was there—the mayor, Rimstad, journalists, the teachers, and the whole school. The water ran out of a tap."

"Did the mayor say something stupid?"

"Oh, I don't remember."

"Well, of course you remember. Think about it."

Jon pretended that he was thinking. Just then the door of the farmhouse opened—the house was some distance away, over by the hill—and Karl's wife, Margrete, came out and stood on the stoop. Her dress shone wine red under the iron gray sky. She crossed her arms over her bosom and shivered, her hair fluttering gently in the wind.

"There's food," muttered Karl without turning around. He had obviously heard the door open.

Jon whipped the camera out and slung it up on his shoulder. Margrete saw it and waved.

"What are you doing?" Karl asked petulantly.

Jon started filming, and without moving his eye from the eyepiece he raised his left arm and waved back.

"Look, now she's waving again."

Karl glared crossly in the direction of the house. His wife was acting like a little girl in the limelight. She laughed, she raised both arms over her head and pranced around like a red flame in the colorless landscape. Suddenly the farmer smiled.

"She's still young," he said elatedly, pointing at her. "Do you see that? Hot damn!"

"Yes," said Jon as he savored the feeling of having cast a spell.

When the show was over he proposed that they go back to the soccer field and the water party. He had no interest in having dinner with Elisabeth and listening to the endless talk about moving plans.

"There's a party at the club," he said.

Karl wasn't so sure. Well, he'd have to get cleaned up.

Karl was in the habit of working when nobody else was doing so, evenings and weekends. That way it looked as if he was unusually industrious.

It turned out to be the biggest party of the season. Jon danced. With Elisabeth and Marit. Hans did *not* dance with Elisabeth. He danced with his wife, and occasionally with Marit when he was able to cut in between Jon and Georg. Paul stuck to Gerd, who cried the whole evening because the project was finished and the divers were going to leave. Karl danced with Margrete as long as she could stay on her feet, and he didn't mention a word about the disgusting Miss Venus that he had hidden in the barn.

There was a lot of drinking but little bickering. The young men who operated the salmon farm on North Island had made up with the divers. It was past 4:00 A.M. when Jon finally stumbled home and went to bed.

He dreamt that he was standing in the soccer field and watching water run out of the pipe. People were so preoccupied with the food and the social activities taking place under the tarpaulins that they had forgotten the water pipe. The water was running out to no purpose, with a gushing sound that grew louder and louder and finally became so deafening that Jon had to run across the field and shut it off—just like somebody would shut off a blaring radio when something important was to be said.

But Jon wasn't just a random somebody, and now he learned that all over again. He had no right to act on behalf of others. They stared at him. They stopped talking. They stopped eating, stopped enjoying themselves, just stood and stared accusingly at him. He was the aching target of the condemnation of an entire community. He had taken from them the lifegiving blood about which the mayor had spoken so warmly.

And it went on and on. He just stood there, immovable, consumed by shame. And it went on and on.

11

He lay in his room dozing, daydreaming, and listening to Elisabeth, who was humming down in the kitchen. He had been staying indoors most of the time since the divers had left. Three days out fishing with Frank was plenty. Jon was no fisherman. He knew what to do, and he liked the product of their efforts, but the days that never came to an end, pitch-black coffee, one dripping net after another, let 'em down and pull 'em up empty, and the endless shrill chatter from the radio in the wheelhouse—no, that was not for him.

He had also gone hunting, but the geese had disappeared. There were some rabbits, but they had not turned white yet and they stayed high in the mountains. He had never been interested in ptarmigans. They were all skin and bones, and constantly flitting about—suitable quarry for Lapps and city folks. He took a couple of walks with Nils, fixed the grindstone and straightened up the fence.

Then it suddenly stopped raining. Fall was over. A thin layer of snow blanketed the green moss. The nights grew longer, soon becoming so long that there was almost no day. Jon was content to just lie and loaf, make up stories in his head, let the digressions lead him through fork after fork in the road until the path became so narrow that it ended by itself, like the uncharted paths in the endless bogs.

A kettle lid clattered down in the kitchen, and Elisabeth stopped humming. He reflected lazily that now something was going to happen. This was the calm before the storm.

90

He heard footsteps on the stairs, a squeak from the unlubricated doorhandle, and Elisabeth came in. He opened his eyes and looked at her, sleepily.

"I just happened to think of something," she said as she sat down on the edge of the bed. "How could you know about that letter?"

Many years of living with Elisabeth had taught Jon to think carefully before responding to such questions.

"The journalist told me," he said.

"That she had sent it, yes. But you knew that it had come?"

"Uh . . . yeah."

He half closed one eyelid in order to concentrate. Could he have somehow spilled the beans as they were walking home from the soccer field that day? Ordinarily he couldn't care less about whether his letters were censored, for he eventually got them anyway. But Marit had planted the fatal idea that there might have been a letter for him that he *didn't* get.

"Do you snoop around in my things to see if I am hiding something from you?" Elisabeth asked.

"Once in awhile," he admitted for the sake of honesty.

"I do it for your own good," she said. "I hope you understand that. That journalist writes about Lisa, and it's not good for you. She's the one that's getting you all mixed up. I know that!"

His eyes were wide open now, and he remained silent.

"It's over two years since she left. You must forget her. She is nothing to you."

"I can't," said Jon. "She is in my head."

"Oh, Jon."

"I've tried. It doesn't work."

It's *got* to work. It always works. If I have to forget Hans then I just *have* to."

"You haven't tried yet."

"I know. But you have to understand that she is a completely different person now. It's hard to take, but . . . well, she clearly has forgotten you. She . . . she . . ."

91

"Yes?" he said coldly, opening his eyes. "Come on, out with it."

"She has a boyfriend," said Elisabeth.

"How do you know that?"

"Oh, one hears things of that sort."

"Where, then?"

"Don't be silly! Everywhere, of course. Surely you know that?"

Jon knew his sister better than he knew anyone else, and this was not a good sign, not so much because of what she said, but because it was impossible to find out if what she said was true. She may have heard rumors in the community, but there may also have been a letter.

"What is it that you have told that journalist?" she asked.

"Nothing."

"She thinks Lisa has disappeared?"

"I guess so."

"Listen to me, Jon. I know good and well that it was a catastrophe for you when Lisa went away, but it would have been no less of a catastrophe if she had stayed here. Quite the contrary, for then you would have had to deal with the problem at close range."

"Like Hans's wife?"

"Don't get smart. That which is painful in life isn't always the result of unfaithfulness. Sometimes it's just that people are different, that their lives don't fit any more, that they each go their own way. As a matter of fact, that is even worse than an overt act. So now I think you should call or write to that journalist and tell her that she is not to bother about this any more, that she should just forget about both you and Lisa."

"That's not necessary."

"She has obviously initiated an investigation of some sort, and it's gotten completely out of hand. What is she looking for?"

"The truth," he said with a smile.

"And what is that, my boy? Whatever suits you? Whatever you want to hear?"

"No," he thought, turning toward the wall. "It's what is right. It's what gives you peace and allows you to sleep."

He curled up in a fetal position and she resignedly stroked his hair—something she almost never did. They lived in the same house, but the only times they normally touched each other was when, right out in public, she took his arm, just in fun.

When she came home from school the next afternoon, he was gone.

12

The bus crawled up the steep incline on the inner side of the island, then glided slowly through the curves as it reached the plateau. It was dark, the snow was falling steadily, but there was no traffic on the road.

As it descended on the other side it went even slower. The snowplows drove by with their warning lights flashing, and the bus driver peered intently into the oscillating colored beams. The interior bus lights were not on. Jon, the only passenger on the bus, was sporting a new jacket and a fresh haircut. He sat on the engine housing and talked about Copenhagen, the big city where the sun continued to shine until late autumn, and where one didn't have to dress any warmer than on an ordinary August day here in the north. The wind didn't blow constantly there, once you combed your hair it stayed combed, and your clothes didn't get ruined by rain and bad weather.

The driver was only half listening.

Down by the bogs they went past two cattle guards and a small grove. They saw a farmyard light far off to the left, the grove receded behind them, and the landscape flattened out to nothingness in the impenetrable darkness.

Suddenly, pointing, the driver said, "Look there!" Jon pressed his face against the windshield. Three or four hundred meters ahead of them, just off the road, they saw car lights shining at a crazy angle. Just then the slush covered the windshield like a gray wall, and they had to stop.

The headlights really were pointing in a strange direction, and they remained stopped.

"Something must have happened," said the driver. Jon agreed. Something was always happening on his island.

The back wheels of the car were in the ditch, and the lights pointed skyward at an oblique angle. A woman was standing in the middle of the road, waving.

Jon jumped out and took hold of her. It was Hans's wife, the nurse. She was inadequately dressed for the weather, wet through and through, and shivering from the cold. Blood was running from a cut under one eye, and it was obvious that she was somewhat disoriented.

He carried her into the bus and placed her on the front passenger seat. The driver removed her shoes and began to massage her feet.

"I want to die," she wailed, twisting her head from side to side. "I want to die."

"All right, now," said the driver. "Are you alone?"

She was in no condition to explain what was going on—she just kept repeating over and over again that she wanted to die—so Jon went out to have a look. He found the car empty. It was the same blue Subaru that he had seen hidden in the woods by Grinda one night long ago. He could see no tracks other than hers in the snow around the car. He turned off the lights and went back to the bus.

"What the hell are you doing out in weather like this?" the driver asked crossly. He was sure she would have died if they hadn't found her.

"He knows!" she whimpered, pointing at Jon.

"Knows what?"

"What I am doing here. He and his sister. They are draining my lifeblood. God, they're draining my lifeblood."

Jon didn't have the slightest idea what she was doing here at this moment, unless it was that she was looking for Hans. He had never liked this woman. He didn't like her constant pouting, her cross-looking face when she scolded her kids, the injured expression that she wore when she sat with her husband at a party, refusing to drink, or flirt, or have any fun—a bitch of a woman who only wanted to go home and stay home and, unfortunately for her, couldn't hold a candle to Elisabeth.

He put his finger under the cut on her face and opened it. She threw her head back and stared wildly at him.

"Don't touch me!"

"It isn't deep," he said as he laid a woolen blanket over her, one that he had stolen on the boat. When she threw it off, he had to quickly step away from her and resist the temptation to slap her. The driver held her down and forcibly wrapped the blanket around her. Her teeth were chattering.

"The car!" she shouted when he started driving. "I need the car to go to work tomorrow."

"To hell with the car!"

"I must have the car, I say!"

Her voice bored into Jon's brain. He had to put his hands over his ears so as not to lose his senses. He was home again, back in the snow and the darkness. The sight of it sent a chill down his spine.

Finally they reached his stop. He kept his head down as he got off, looking neither at the driver nor at the prostrate woman. He carried his baggage through the deep snow. He knew exactly what lay ahead of him: an empty house, dark windows through which he could see the pale beams of the yard light casting shadows on the drifted snow, the endless lapping of the waves upon the shore in the darkness beyond. He had taken this trip in order to restore a balance, and then he came home to this!

He dug the ladder out of the snow, climbed in the attic window, and from there made his way down into the house. He left his boots and his baggage standing just inside the door so Elisabeth would see that he was home and not get frightened. He built a fire, set up the video camera, and sat back in the armchair.

"I'm home again," he said.

Immediately Lisa was there. Her voice hit him like a jet of ice

96

water. She was standing by the old lawn furniture behind the house at the fish works, clad in a yellow and white cotton dress with tiny little violets, white knee socks, and red shoes that looked striking against the lush, green grass. Pigtails with green ribbons, and in her hand a piece of cake. It was the 22nd of May, and it was bright and sunny.

"The camera," he thought, turning to one side.

She was ten years old. She held the piece of cake up high for all to see and acted as if she were an ordinary ten-year-old having her picture taken on a special day. Jon smiled. He was also ten years old. He wasn't supposed to be there, but he *was* there, hidden in the bushes, ready to squeeze the shutter. He squeezed it and immediately ducked down.

Elisabeth stood in the doorway and looked at him. Her sweater and slacks were wet. Her hair was wet. Drops of water sparkled in her eyelashes.

"So you got a haircut?" she said, turning off the camera. He bent his head forward so she could see the white spots under his ears and on his neck, just like he used to do when he came from the barber as a boy. "Where have you been?"

"In Copenhagen."

"Copenhagen? Well, well."

It was such a preposterous lie that it didn't even register. She held her hands close to the fire and was momentarily preoccupied. He thought she was prettier than ever, loved by a man whom he hated, but who satisfied her.

"She drove in the ditch," he said. Then he told her about Hans's wife, leaving out a few things and adding a few others so it wouldn't sound too reproachful, yet without sounding indifferent. In a way, the episode had made him realize something of the seriousness of what his sister was doing.

"It doesn't surprise me" was all she said, for she was already so deeply involved that she was incapable of caring about anything except her own interests in the matter.

97

"Have there been any letters for me?" he asked after a short pause. She had found a hairbrush and was standing in front of the fireplace getting the snarls out of her hair.

"No."

"And nobody has called?"

She chuckled. "Who would ever think of calling here?"

"Georg, for example?"

"No, he hasn't called. And there haven't been any letters either. Now, where have you *really* been?"

"In Copenhagen."

She rolled her eyes toward the ceiling in disbelief.

"You're getting worse and worse. And I suppose you didn't have your medicine with you either, did you?"

He thought it a little strange that a sister, his nearest and, indeed, only family, didn't exhibit greater concern about the fact that he had been away so long, and that he had left without warning. But it was possible that she was just hiding her concern.

"Couldn't you cook some coffee?" he asked.

"But it's in the middle of the night."

"What difference does that make?"

"It would keep you awake."

"Cocoa, then?"

"No."

"Well, so be it."

Maybe it wasn't so unusual. Wasn't she always self-centered like this when she came home after a night with Hans?

He stood up and was going to leave, but in the light from the kitchen she noticed that he was wearing a new jacket. And not just any new jacket: it was expensive and modern, not at all like those he normally ordered from a catalog.

"Where have you been?" she asked again, much more seriously than before.

"In Copenhagen," he said for the third time.

She suddenly became furious, threw the hairbrush against the wall and grabbed him by the collar.

"Stop that nonsense!" she yelled. "Now answer me: *Where have you been?*"

He composed himself, looked her right in the eyes without blinking, as he always did when a well-hidden truth was finally to be revealed.

"Is it true?" she asked, astonished.

"It's true."

"What were you doing there?"

"Looking for Lisa."

"*Looking for Lisa? In Copenhagen?*"

She couldn't believe him, but what followed was no ordinary quarrel. She got tears in her eyes, and when she mumbled, "Poor boy," her voice was both gentle and compassionate.

She rubbed her hand over his newly barbered hair, as if this and the new jacket were the visible proofs that he had gone completely to the dogs.

"And I thought you were out at the cabin."

Karl owned an old shack by a lake in the mountains where Jon occasionally spent the night when his hunting trips got too long for him to make it home by nightfall.

"It can't be true," she said. "You can't make me believe just anything. You may be crazy, but *I'm* not. Not yet, anyway."

He sat down again.

"Can you cook coffee?" he asked again.

"No, I said."

Outdoors they heard the gentle swish of melting snow sliding down the roof. A winter that began like this would begin many times. The snow that fell tonight would disappear tomorrow or the next day. In a few days there would be another foot or two, and that would also melt. It would take turns raining and snowing until the wind and freezing temperature would finally lay a brown crust over the island and make it possible for the snow to stay on the ground.

99

Jon went out to the front hall and got his luggage.

"I bought something for you," he said. He pulled out two plates: Royal Danish porcelain, in blue—sky blue, iron blue, and many other shades of blue in a pattern that Elisabeth at one time would have given her eyeteeth to own. But in his zeal to find the right proof, he had forgotten about the fact that Royal Danish was associated with a time when there was still some life in her marriage—a time when Elisabeth was *happy*. That messed up the picture.

She took one plate in each hand and stared breathlessly at them. "I think I'm going crazy," she said. "Okay, I give up. You *have* been away."

"In Copenhagen."

"All right, in Copenhagen. And I thought you were in the mountains."

It was hard to say why she cried, but his guns stood as always in the corner by the door, where they had been the entire time that he was gone, and he never went to the mountains without them. Never. The same thing happened with Lisa that time that *she* ran off to Copenhagen. Time went by, day after day, and nobody went searching for her.

13

"What does one do to find something?" Jon wrote, filling in vacant squares from top to bottom in an old crossword puzzle that he hadn't been able to solve. Then, horizontally, he wrote: "One digs and digs, brushes it off and looks at it, maybe it can be used for something..." Perhaps one finds peace again. But he found none.

When the weather calmed down and the snow melted, he got busy once again. He took his last few crowns out of the bank and bought siding for the rotting south wall, asphalt shingles, builder's paper, insulation, and lathing, as he had been planning to do for several years. He arranged for it all to be delivered to the house, and when Elisabeth came home from school he was busily at work.

"Now the house will be warmer," he hollered from the ladder.

She scarcely looked at the wall. She was carrying a woolen blanket, the one he had stolen on the boat and later placed around Hans's wife when he found her freezing on the road.

"What is the meaning of this?" she asked angrily.

"That's my blanket," he said.

"So it really is true. And where, if I may ask, did you get it?"

"I stole it on the boat."

"And gave it to her?"

"She was freezing to death."

"If only that were true. Can you imagine how I felt when that hussy came strutting into the classroom and gave it to me in front of everybody?"

No, Jon couldn't imagine that. A woolen blanket? Was that anything to hand over in front of everybody? Once again he had to acknowledge that there were many things in Elisabeth's world that he didn't understand. Moreover, it irritated him that his sister was getting more and more like her lover's pathetic wife.

"You're just grousing," he said as he applied the wrecking bar to an old stud.

She began to chew him out, far more vehemently than the situation warranted. And when he came down to fetch a lath, she went so far as to grab him by the arm. How could he think of giving the damn blanket to that wretched woman? "You did it just to make a fool of me!" she snarled. "Just admit it!"

He stared dumbfounded.

Then he reached into the pile of new building material with the wrecking bar, and she finally took notice of what he was doing.

"What in the world do you think you are doing?" she shrieked, then added without a pause: "We're going to be moving!"

"*I'm* not moving," he said.

"Yes, you are, even if I have to take you out of here by force in a police car. How much do you think this costs?"

"It's my money."

"Your money? Which we could have used in our new flat. To hell with you, Jon!"

"What did you mean about the police car?"

"To hell with you," I said.

"What did you mean about the police car?"

"To hell with you."

He picked up a stapler that he was planning to use to fasten the paper to the wall, pressed it against the back of his hand, and pulled the trigger. The staple slammed into the flesh between his thumb and forefinger and stuck there.

"You're crazy," she mumbled, backing away.

"Yes," he said. "And I will never leave this place. *Never!* Do you hear me?"

He didn't expect an answer. He stuck the tip of his sheath knife under the staple and pulled it out again. Two rivulets of blood trickled down over his skin, coming together at the wrist.

"You're crazy," she mumbled again and hurried into the house.

He remained standing and looked around. His whole family had lived here. He wondered if this was his grandfather's legend all over again, if *his* struggle to remain here was dimly reflected in Jon's. The old man was the family's model and hero. He built the railroad and fished for herring, laid the hay over the drying racks and fathered many children. His name was all over the place—in the membership lists at the Youth Club, the debtors' registry, the columns of the local newspaper, and on the monument by the little gray church listing those who fought in the war. He could repair a pocket watch just as skillfully as he could rig a mast or slaughter a cow. He was in debt throughout his life and well into that of his son, Jon's uncle, who never got out from under it and finally had to divide up the farm and turn the family into fishermen and day laborers.

There was only one extant picture of the old man, and it hung in Jon's room. There, however, he was *not* working, whereas the legend said he always was. But in the picture he was lying in the shade of a hay-drying rack and sleeping, with his head resting on the neck of a horse, which was also sleeping. "Grandfather resting," the picture was called. It had hung there since long before Jon was born, long before he had been told that everything was interconnected, without interruption—the old and the new, the mother who hummed in the kitchen twenty years ago and Elisabeth who did so today, the father who came home from Lofoten and Jon who came home from the mountains. They hung their coats and caps in the same entryway, put their boots in the same hall, tarred the same boat, turned the crank on the same grindstone. The afternoon sun shone reddish yellow on the black tar paper on the wall where Jon had stripped off the old siding: it, too, was a continuation of the old wall and the beginning of a new one. The bare mountain ash trees that Grandfather had planted, the willows with spring slumbering under their bark that had always stood there along the path leading to the sea . . . No, Jon was not made of the same stuff as his grandfather. He was the continuation, to be sure, but the things he spent his time on didn't amount to anything. He just did whatever he felt like doing at the moment. There was no plan, no vision. He struggled against his sister, not against starvation, big business, and Hitler. Some struggle, that. Woolen blankets? Absurdity must be an invention of our time. At least there wasn't anything about it in the municipal records, so presumably it was one of the many modern signs of doomsday—along with the atom bombs.

Elisabeth came out on the doorstep again in a gesture of reconciliation. She held one hand over her eyes to shield them from the daylight.

"The TV is working," she shouted up to him.

"I know," he said crossly. "The antenna was the first thing I fixed."

It could have been just an ordinary day. The smell of fresh coffee wafted out through the open door. The sunlight had grown dimmer, the marshes faded slowly into the haze as they always did at this time of the year. But Jon had to admit that something had come to an end. The erosion was grinding and grinding beneath the surface—and it was going to win.

A yellow Mercedes appeared in the distance. It went down the hill, through the little wooded area, and on toward Jon and Elisabeth's house. It drove slowly, as if to give any passengers an opportunity to enjoy the view.

It stopped in the yard and the driver hopped out. It was the sheriff. He was alone and looked sporty and young in his Icelandic sweater and hunting boots. His hair was a bit thinner than it had been in the days when he and Elisabeth were schoolmates, but he still had the same mischievous look and the same virile movements. A three-day beard covered his face.

"Well, so it's you!" said Elisabeth, blushing.

They had once been more than classmates, and it was a long time since they had seen each other. She didn't know whether he was there on official business or monkey business. "Have you finally come to court me?" she asked.

"Don't I wish!" he laughed as he looked back and forth between her and Jon, who was up on the ladder. "Actually, I've just come to have a few words with that fellow."

"With Jon?"

He nodded.

"Hear that, Jon? Erik wants to talk to you!"

"I hear. What does he want?"

"Just a little chat. Are you coming?"

"I'd rather not. I'm busy."

"Come on down, boy, or I'll tip the ladder. Ha ha."

"Well, okay."

"Can we go in the house?" Elisabeth asked.

Jon realized that he wasn't going to get any more work done today. He packed up his tools, spread a tarp over the materials, and took down the ladder. Then he was ready for whatever he was supposed to be ready for.

The sheriff took plenty of time getting down to business. He rolled a cigarette and listened to Elisabeth's reports about things at school and her account of their moving plans, including a long description of the flat they were going to live in. They talked about the new water and about a farmer—not Karl this time—who had lost four sheep in the mountains. Finally he turned to Jon.

"Well, Jon," he said, "I'm told that you've been bothering old Sakkariassen at night. Is that true?"

The house suddenly became very quiet.

"No," said Jon.

"He says that you stand in the darkness near his house and stare in through the windows. He wants it to stop."

105

Elisabeth looked at her brother.

"Is that true?"

"No. It's not me."

Jon was used to getting blamed for things like this, although it usually wasn't the sheriff who brought the accusation. Sometimes he had done something crazy, sometimes not—like this time.

"Listen here," the sheriff went on. "We know that you hunt without a license, we know that you shoot your rifle most anywhere you please. But we don't do anything about those things, because there'd be no end to it if we went after people for every little infraction. But Sakkariassen is an old man. He is lying up in his little room and isn't long for this world. What good does it do to hassle him?"

"It's not me," Jon said once again.

"Last night, between two and three in the morning?"

"No."

"So you think the old man is just seeing things?"

"I have no idea."

The sheriff had the biggest fists Jon had ever seen. He placed one of his own alongside the sheriff's: it looked puny by comparison. They smiled.

"Okay. Then Elisabeth certainly can confirm what you are saying?"

"No. She wasn't here."

"Wasn't here?"

"She was out with Hans."

Erik sat up straighter and looked steadily at Elisabeth.

"With Hans?" he laughed. "That tomcat! I thought you had better sense than that."

Elisabeth grimaced.

"Why don't you try *me* instead?" he asked.

"Because you're married and have two kids," said Jon.

They laughed.

"Jon, you're a pig."

He looked at the floor.

"I also heard that his wife tried to commit suicide," said the sheriff. "So that was all because of you. Not bad, eh?"

She threw a washrag at him, so he had to stand up and grab her around the waist with those huge fists of his.

"I'm leaving," said Jon, getting up.

"He has reported you, Jon," the sheriff called after him. "Let that be a warning."

"Yeah, yeah."

Some crows flew by in the windless evening, enroute to the hills. The eider ducks' muffled quacking sounded from the bay, and a cow bellowed in a barn off in the distance.

Jon began to pull nails out of the old boards. He pulled out the sawhorse and placed it so as to catch the light from the cellar door. He was thinking about how fragile life was on this earth. One comes to a point in life where one does everything one can to preserve what is best—and then one is unable to live with the result. He had resisted the threat from the divers—at least he had managed to push that away. He had resisted the threat from Elisabeth—for the moment. Then Sakkariassen came into the picture. Was this a new threat, or just an ordinary bit of fussing by a crazy, isolated old man?

He sawed up one pile of wood after another and carried it, armload by armload, into the cellar. Finally, out in the yard, he heard the Mercedes start up and drive away. By then it was late in the evening.

Elisabeth had a bone to pick with him. It was disloyal to tell the sheriff that she wasn't home at night.

"I was home," he said in a perplexed attempt to stick to the essentials.

"I know that," she cut him off. "You don't ever go anywhere. But why do you go out any time someone comes here—just to make a point?"

He pretended he hadn't heard her.

107

"You sit down there in the cellar and feel lonely, isn't that so?"

"Uh . . . , yeah, I guess so."

"Just to make me feel guilty?"

Guilt was the rope that bound her firmly to him and that now and then threatened to strangle her.

"No," he said, "that isn't why I do it."

"Why, then?"

"I chop wood—bang, bang, bang, bang . . ."

He banged the pot lid against his chair and smiled.

"Don't try to change the subject by being flippant about it. Not home at night? How could you say such a thing?"

He realized that all this grousing had nothing to do with him— neither the squabble over the woolen blanket nor his staying in the cellar. Obviously there must be some problem or other with Hans again.

The only thing in the kettle was some overcooked potatoes, and there was no indication that there were any plans for dinner. He was hungry, but he went outside again anyway and stayed out until night came and Elisabeth left for another rendezvous with her lover. Then he gobbled down a couple slices of bread, put on a dark jacket and hat, dark pants and black boots and stuck a spray can with red paint in his pocket.

It was past midnight, and there was no moon. A thin layer of frost covered the clay road. The village was dark and quiet, with scattered yard lights that shone like phosphorescence in a slumbering sea.

He stayed off the main street, detoured around the post office and the clubhouse, continued on across the soccer field where the pipe with the new water still poked up out of the gravel, and sneaked over to the back of the school. There, using the spray can, he wrote in big block letters on the wall, both inside the schoolyard and on the outside facing the street: LISA LIVES NO MORE. He wrote the same thing between two cola ads on a nearby kiosk, on the foundation of the supermarket, and on the wooden fence beyond it. Then he slipped into the empty field at the edge of the village.

He knew the paths north of the village like the back of his hand. An hour later he stood in the yard of the farm behind the fish works and threw stones against the window of Sakkariassen's bedroom. The light came on, and the old man could be seen through the window. At first he was just a fleeting shadow, but Jon continued to throw stones, and eventually the window flew open.

"Is someone there?" he shouted.

Jon waited until he had shouted three times. Then he took off his hat and stood in the light.

"It's me," he said.

The old eyes narrowed in anger. He recognized the intruder, opened his mouth and backed away. Jon heard a thump and a shout, and almost a minute passed before the man reappeared at the window.

"What do you want of me?" he shouted huskily.

Jon didn't want anything, at least not anything that he felt like stating at the moment. Scare you into doing something, he could have answered, but that would have been only half the truth. He put his hat back on and receded into the shadows.

The old man continued shouting, almost in fear. The lights came on in the first floor as well. The door opened, and the cooper from whom Jon had bought the barrel came out in his underwear. He stood under Sakkariassen's window and asked what was going on.

"There's somebody there," said Sakkariassen meekly.

Jon had moved way out to the edge of the yard and laid down under a bush. The smell of crushed currant twigs mingled with rotten kelp and fish scraps from the wharf. This time when Lisa appeared beside him it was not to torment him but to share his delight. He heard the cooper's gruff voice:

"And who might it be?"

"That crazy kid. He was here again."

Yes, Jon thought to himself, he had been here his whole life, to the sorrow and torment of that old pig.

"I saw him with my own eyes. Right where you are standing now."

The cooper put his hands on his hips and looked around, walked dutifully around the yard for a bit, and peeked under a few bushes. He saw nothing. And the only sounds that could be heard were the usual ones, the ones that belonged there—the sea, and the gulls clawing in the corrugated iron roof where they were roosting. Jon hadn't made any sounds when he was here before, and he didn't make any now either.

"I don't see anything," said the cooper as he headed for the door.

"He's there. I swear it."

"No, I say. There's nobody here. Go back to bed!"

That was really something new. Nobody talked like that to Sakkariassen, not even the cooper, when he was in his prime. Jon wondered if he might not be right in assuming that the old man had lost his grip on things. When the cooper had closed the door and turned out the light on the first floor, Jon stood up and resumed his position under the window.

Sakkariassen looked right at him for twenty seconds, maybe half a minute.

"I see that you are there," he muttered. "I see that you are there."

Then he closed the window with a bang.

Jon ran through the yard and leaped over the fence. The voices followed him as he raced southward over the moss-covered stones. There were more of them now, the cooper and two or three other men, all engaged in a rancorous argument with the old man staring defiantly out the window. But it didn't concern him; he was out of range, and content, as if he had carried out a complicated order and done it to perfection.

110

14

He worked on the wall for three days. Then another storm blew in and lasted for over a day, and the following morning he had to go out with Frank to search for some nets that had washed out to sea during the storm.

They dragged the area and found a few scraps of line here and there, but nothing of any value, and by early afternoon they had to take shelter from yet another storm. They secured the motorboat at the dock and sat around for awhile with some other fishermen on the rattan chairs at the Cooperative Society. Frank bought a round of beer, and they talked about the weather and the damage done by the storm. The others had also lost some fishing gear.

Jon didn't listen very closely. Through the steamed-up window he could see green letters that had been sprayed on the telephone booth outside the school, though the message could not be read from this distance.

"Yes, it's crazy," Frank said derisively. He was talking about the new water. "It came this far and no farther."

He was referring to the school.

"Not only is it too expensive, but now the Conservative Party is opposing it because the municipality would have to exercise the power of eminent domain over some private property."

"The Center Party, too," said one of the fishermen who was also a member of the municipal council. "They're against it because the farmers say the Waterworks ruins the drainage ditches."

"What is that over there on the telephone booth?" Jon asked, poking Frank in the ribs. The painted letters made him restless.

The young man leaned forward in his chair and rubbed moisture from the window to improve his view. He still couldn't read it. "No doubt just some bullshit some kids have written," he said.

"Doesn't it say something about Lisa?"

"Lisa who? No, I can't see what it says."

He continued talking about the new water, which now was threatening to plunge the municipality into a budget shortfall and other problems—if one was to believe the newspapers and the local radio station. There was even talk of sending the mayor down to Oslo to ask the government for a handout.

Jon was completely confused.

"Is that Elisabeth coming over there?" he asked fearfully, as if his senses threatened to betray him.

"It sure as hell is," said Frank, looking outside again. "Sure, it's her, can't you see that? What's wrong with you? You look sick."

Sick? He felt pretty much like he had felt when he saw the shadow under the divers' boat, and when he stood in the newspaper office in the city and suddenly realized that he couldn't trust his own visual impressions.

He picked up the bag with the groceries and boxes of nails— there weren't even any lintels on the old wall—and left.

His sister came running toward him, took his arm and acted carefree and happy like she used to do when he came home safely from the sea.

"We'll go home together," she said. "I have something to tell you. Hans says he will get a divorce. What do you think of that?"

Nothing could have pleased him less. He stared at the enormous letters. They were so incredibly *real*.

"It's not the first time," she continued, "and I probably can't depend on it this time either, but . . . well, I can't stop hoping. Can you understand that?"

"No."

"God, to think that one can be so preoccupied with a man. Ten years ago I didn't give men a second thought, or else I took them for granted, I don't remember which. All I cared about then was politics, my education, and all the wonderful things I was going to accomplish when I was ready. Now all I can think about is . . . Jon, listen to me!"

"Uh, oh, okay."

"We could put an end to all this difficulty and live like normal human beings. And you're the one it mainly affects. Do you remember when Mama died and we were left alone? You were just a little fellow, but I couldn't stand you. I pretended that I didn't see what happened that time when you fell in the well . . ."

They had reached the place where the school buses were waiting. The children were streaming out of the schoolyard. Elisabeth smiled and waved. "It will certainly be sad to leave them. Yes, I think of them almost as if they were my own. Perhaps I like this island better than I realize. Oh, Jon, I hope you never have to go through anything like this—*knowing* that people are deceiving you and then trusting them anyway because you *have* to. It's awful."

Jon read aloud from the concrete wall that Lisa was no longer living. "*Green* letters," he thought to himself.

"Yes, isn't that macabre?" said Elisabeth. "We talked about it at the teachers' meeting today. Surely you're not the one who has done it—after all the talking you've been doing about Lisa lately?"

"No."

"I didn't think so. It was suggested that the matter be reported, but a majority decided that we should just remove it and say nothing about it. People who do things like that only get worse if one makes a big fuss about it."

They were engulfed in a flock of children who were going the same direction as they were. A little girl took Elisabeth's hand and started telling a dramatic story about a jump-rope in the schoolyard.

Jon stopped in bewilderment. He gave his sister the bag of gro-

113

ceries and told her to go on ahead. Then he ran back to the telephone booth and dialed the number of the sheriff's office. There was no answer. As it continued to ring he looked through the letters on the window—they looked backwards from inside, he noted—and saw Elisabeth cross the road, she and her children. He vomited. Twice.

Then he dialed the number again. Still no luck. He tried another number. Finally the sheriff answered.

"Has Sakkariassen reported me again?" he asked breathlessly.

It took awhile before the sheriff could collect his thoughts. This was his home number and he presumably had just gotten up from the dinner table.

"No," he said. "Why should he? Have you been there again?"

"No."

"Well, then, what do you want?"

Jon wasn't sure. All he could do was repeat the question. The sheriff breathed disgustedly into the mouthpiece.

"He has withdrawn his complaint," he said. "Is that what you wanted to ask me about?"

"Uh ... yes."

"Without giving any reason. Surely you haven't threatened him?"

"No."

"Well, I sure hope not. I don't like it that you lie to me, Jon."

"I'm not lying."

"Well, what's this all about, then?"

Again Jon had no answer.

"Are you also the one that has messed up the walls over by the school?"

"No."

"Listen here, Jon. I don't know if you have bothered the old man or not, and it doesn't make any difference now that he has withdrawn the complaint. But I suggest that you go home and talk with Elisabeth. Tell her what's bothering you. She understands you."

He did not go home. He went northward on the main road, out of the village and away from other human beings. He noticed that the leech hills on the fallow fields looked like rusty balls of barbed wire. Some grayish-black piles of hay were still lying in the soggy fields. A calf stood bellowing in the slush. Here and there lay the remains of a wrecked car. This isn't how life ought to be. He couldn't stand it any longer.

He ran out into the field, then turned southward and continued until he was by the municipal building and the doctor's office. The doctor was in street clothes when he came out, just leaving for home.

Out of breath, Jon said, "I don't see well."

"Don't *see* well?"

But the doctor didn't laugh. Jon wasn't one of the hypochondriacs, nor was he a man who went to the doctor just for the fun of it. The few times he had been there he had been *dragged* there. "We'll go inside," he said.

Jon remembered something from that very forenoon. He had been out on the sea with his second cousin looking for fishing gear, but he hadn't *seen* anything, not a single buoy marker. It was Frank who saw everything—what little they found.

"Presumably it was also Frank who knew where to look?" said the doctor. Jon had to admit that that was the case.

He stood back of a line on the floor and read the letters on the screen at the other end of the office. He could see all of them—with one eye, with two eyes—even the w's and z's on the bottom line. They sat down again.

"How do you feel otherwise? Do you still have migraines?"

"No, almost never."

"Are you able to sleep?"

"Yes."

"Do you take your medicine?"

He wrinkled his brow. There had been many doctors here through the years, and they had varying opinions about the use of drugs. Jon couldn't quite remember what answer this one preferred.

"Uh . . . no," he finally said.

"And you get along fine without them?"

"Yeah."

"Good. We have plenty of people here who misuse drugs. What is it you want to tell me, Jon? Get right to the point."

He wasn't here to make his confession, just to assure himself that he could believe what he saw with his own eyes. Now he grabbed his chance.

"I forget things."

"For example?"

He tried to explain. Little things from the last two years. His childhood, his youth, the years at the fish works and out fishing— those he remembered clearly, also the surrounding landscape, and faces and events from those earlier years. But the last two years had gotten all mixed up. Things that happened during this period had disappeared and then reappeared in the strangest order and contexts.

"Shock symptoms," said the doctor, shrugging his shoulders. "Have you experienced something sad—about two years ago, say?"

Jon couldn't think of anything except that it was then that Lisa ran off to Copenhagen and later moved away from the island, but he didn't say anything about that to the doctor.

"I see here in the medical record that my predecessor identified you as depressed. He wanted to get you to a specialist, but apparently you didn't want to do that?"

Jon nodded.

"We're going to be moving," he said.

"Oh, really. Is that sad?"

116

"Yes. And . . ."

"Keep talking. I'm here to listen to that sort of thing."

"Elisabeth doesn't want me along."

"What? That's nonsense! Of course she wants you along."

"Well, maybe. But I'm in the way."

"All of us are in the way now and then. Believe me. But I can't imagine that she doesn't want . . ."

"She's going to get married."

"Aha! And you don't like the guy?"

"No."

"Nor he you?"

"No."

"I can't exactly say that it's unusual either. Is this what is really bothering you?"

No, the real reason he came here was to hear that he was perfectly healthy.

The doctor assured him with a chuckle that in that case he was an exception to the rule. He was swamped with people who were convinced that they were sick, who knew precisely what was wrong with them and exactly what they had to have to be healthy again.

"Of course we could give you a general examination, but to be honest with you . . ."

Jon left.

Elisabeth was a bit melancholy that evening, plagued by second thoughts. She said she feared the consequences of what she had initiated—if, contrary to what she expected, Hans really did leave his wife for her.

They drank some cocoa and were almost like a family again, she with her knitting in her lap, he in the rocking chair staring at his palms. He looked intently at the creases, filled with grime, and wondered what fate was written in their pattern.

"Lisa is dead," he mumbled cautiously.

"Nonsense. It's not true even if it is written on the walls."

"How do you know?"

"Dear Jon, you mustn't let yourself be frightened by that sort of thing."

"The divers found something in Long Lake last fall. It might have been her."

This was clearly off the wall, but he lived in a constant state of restlessness, torn to shreds, so this was nothing but a reflex action.

"Now you're talking pure nonsense," she said calmly. "It's just a macabre joke. And I wouldn't give two cents for those shadows you may have seen in Long Lake. Grandpa also used to see shadows in Long Lake, don't you remember? They thought a sea serpent lived there. He was even interviewed about it on the radio once."

"Yes, but . . ."

"And you have a pretty wild imagination. Do you remember when the roof blew off Karl's barn and landed on the road? You thought the whole island was going to be destroyed—that it was an atomic war, or doomsday, or God knows what."

"I was only ten years old then."

"You were *fifteen*. It was the summer after you were confirmed."

"No, it wasn't in the summertime. It was in November . . ."

"It was in July! Right in the middle of haying. The haydrying racks blew into the sea, don't you remember?"

Yes, as a matter of fact he did remember that.

"And Lisa is alive and doing just fine. It's not more than a couple of months since I saw her. She had to leave the island because she couldn't get along with her father—or with anyone else, for that matter—so now she is living with some relatives down south. You've just got to get that into your head. You're grown up now. Life isn't a crime film. For the most part it's boring, ordinary . . ."

They could hear the dripping in the eaves troughs outside. Elisabeth's knitting needles made a soothing, rustling sound, and the old clock on the wall kept ticking in its usual hypnotic way.

Returning to everyday matters, Jon said: "Karl wants me to help him round up the sheep again this year."

"Really? Is he planning to pay you?"

"Nah."

"It doesn't surprise me. Do you know what he charged to pull Hans's car out of the ditch?"

"No."

"Three hundred crowns! That SOB. So I think you should consider yourself too good to work free for that man. He has plenty of money."

Elisabeth was right. He had dozens of cows and steers, a big check each year from the environmental preservation fund, a lot of under-the-table income on which he paid no taxes, not to mention the compensation he had managed to wangle out of the municipality for the right to run the water pipes across his land.

All things considered, Karl was better off than most of the farmers on the island—despite the fact that his farm looked like a wreck.

As Jon went to bed that night his thoughts turned to Georg. It bothered him that the diver hadn't written to him. It was over a month now since he had left, and the silence had continued longer than Jon could find any reasonable explanation for.

15

From the knoll at the foot of the mountain he could see the whole community, the houses here and there on the northern part of the island and the archipelago stretching endlessly into the distance. Jon was out to help round up the sheep—not to earn money, for Karl wouldn't give him a nickel, but to get away from home. The moving plans were shifting into high gear. Elisabeth was starting to pack—a picture here, a lamp there—from the time she came home from work until she went to bed. Slowly but surely she was removing his familiar world from walls and tables, stuffing it down into gray boxes that stood around and turned their home into a warehouse.

He had finally gotten paid for the work he had done on Long Lake, and in his desperation had bought siding for the west wall as well. But it was too late. Elisabeth would no longer let herself be dissuaded by "meaningless" expenditures.

"Go jump in the lake," she said, laughing in his face. The decision was *final.*

So he went to the mountains. Here he could at least put some melancholy distance between himself and the community that was being torn from him. Things were quiet down there now. The fishing was done for the year, the herring all packed in spices and salt and stored behind the fish works. The grazing season was over, and the fish business and the work on the water project were at a standstill. It was autumn. There was a little wet snow, but in every direction he could see brown fields and dark mountains.

He closed his eyes, laid his head against the knoll, and knew that he would have been a happy man if his childhood home were not being annihilated. The shadow was out of his head, and he no longer was having hallucinations. He could enjoy the laziness of autumn and winter, even the association with Karl and those ragged sheep of his. He could knock his head cautiously against the stone and just be in the world—and that's all he would need.

A little sand and gravel slid down into the ravine below. He heard a shout and the sound of running feet. When he opened his eyes he saw movement in the birch branches on the ridge on the other side of the ravine.

Near a brook running through a thicket in the ravine he met two other young people—Kari, who had been with Georg at the party, and Trond, one of the farm workers, who was standing and poking a wet bundle that lay on the ground between them. It was some clothing, tied together around a handbag that Jon immediately recognized.

"What in the world is it?" Kari asked apprehensively.

"A woman's coat and a handbag," said Trond.

"Yuck!" she said, "Leave it be, and let's just go on. I'm sure there are sheep farther up."

"I found it right here, under that stone." He pointed to a small cave under a moss-covered slab of rock.

"That was nothing to shout about. Now Jon is coming too. What's that to be afraid of, a pile of clothing?"

"I wasn't afraid. I just think it's . . . repulsive."

Jon peered into the cave. It was big enough so that a person could crawl in and be completely hidden from view. He wondered if he had ever been here before.

"Put it down," said Kari in a nagging tone of voice. "Let's just go on."

"It's Lisa's," said Jon. Trond dropped the bundle. No doubt he was thinking of the writing on the walls down in the village.

All at once Karl came sliding down the steep slope and asked why they were just standing there. Nobody answered.

Jon picked up the wet bundle and opened the handbag. It contained a pink comb, a broken mirror, a small bag of sticky candy, and a plastic billfold that was discolored by the moisture. There was no sign of rust on the clasp or the handle, no evidence of rotting in either the lining of the handbag or the clothing. It couldn't have been lying there for more than a couple of months at most.

"How do you know that it's . . . hers?" asked Kari, and Jon noticed that she didn't want to say Lisa's name.

"I recognize it," he said. "It's her comb."

"A comb like that could belong to anybody," said Trond.

"Yuck!" said Kari once again. "How can you touch that stuff!"

"Why shouldn't I touch it?" Her trepidation irritated him.

"Haven't you seen what the kids have been writing on the walls down in the village?" said Karl. "It says LISA IS DEAD."

"It's not the kids," said Jon.

"Really? Well, who is it, then? Grownups certainly don't do things like that."

Jon looked at the clothes. A pair of slacks, a coat, and a sweater that he knew she had knitted herself. They were real and present in the same surprisingly simple way that the writing on the walls was real and present.

"It doesn't bother me to touch it," he mumbled. "It seems completely natural. I can even comb my hair with it. Look."

He pulled the comb through his hair a couple of times, but Karl leaped over to him and grabbed it away.

"Are you out of your mind, boy?" he shouted. "This is no joke. What if she's lying around here somewhere?"

Jon laughed. "Why would she be lying around here?" he asked.

"Well, the clothing is here."

"Yes, just think . . ." said Kari.

Karl said, "Have you ever seen a dead body? No, Jon, you haven't. But I have, and let me tell you: they stink. Do any of you smell anything? A foul smell?"

"I want to get away from here," said Kari. "Trond! Please?"

"No," said Trond. "She may be in there." He nodded toward the cave under the stone. "We better have a look."

"I agree," said Karl. He looked down at the comb he had taken away from Jon and wondered what to do with it. Jon took it back and put it in the handbag.

"I'll go in," he said.

"No, no," said Kari. "Not you. Don't do it, anybody . . . Let's just go home and tell the sheriff what we've seen. Look at Jon—don't you see how weird he looks? Are you scared, Jon?"

Jon didn't feel either weird or scared. Karl looked at him closely.

"No," Karl decided, "there's nothing wrong with him. Is there, Jon?"

Jon shook his head.

"*You're* the one who is afraid, Kari, not us."

"No, no, he's not well, I tell you. I can *see* it. And besides, I don't want to be here any longer."

"Well, go home then."

"Alone? Not on your life. Trond?"

"Forget it. We can't go until we have taken a look."

"I'll do it," said Jon.

"There you see. Jon isn't afraid, are you, Jon?"

"Nah."

"Don't do it, Jon! Don't do it!"

"Shut up!" he bellowed. "I said I would do it, and I will. *I'm going to do it!*"

It got very quiet. After everyone had revealed their fear it was time to give curiosity its due. Trond smiled uncertainly, Karl nodded slowly, and Kari silently bit her red-polished fingernails.

123

If I'm going to be the one that finds her, then so be it Jon thought to himself, looking around furtively. Then he got down on his hands and knees and crept into the cave.

It was not deep—not more than seven or eight meters, an empty hole in the side of the mountain—and once his eyes had adjusted to the darkness it was evident that there was nothing to see, just wet sand and gravel, a damp, greenish rock wall and a few rotting leaves that had been blown in by the wind.

"There's nothing there," he said as he came out.

They looked at him as he brushed the sand from his clothes, and suddenly they were dubious. They were no longer afraid, not even Kari, and the disappointment was palpable.

"Nothing?"

"No, nothing."

They glanced questioningly at each other—embarrassed, perhaps, that they had allowed themselves to get so upset over a few articles of clothing and a little pink comb.

"Well, I'm going to have a look myself," said Karl crossly as he got down on all fours and crawled into the dark opening. He was gone just a few seconds before he came out again, red with anger.

"And just what is this?" he roared, shoving two new items of clothing into Jon's face. "Can you tell me that?"

A scarf. Lisa's. And a shirt, also Lisa's.

He grabbed his head. "No!" he said. Then—skeptically, despairingly—"I didn't see them. They weren't there!"

"But of course they were there. I found them!"

"No, no . . ."

"Come on, be reasonable! Do you think I plucked them out of thin air?"

"Now I *really* don't want to be here any longer," said Kari, starting down toward the village. But nobody paid any attention to her, and she stopped after going a few steps.

"And the body?" said Trond maliciously. "There must have been a body in all these clothes?"

124

"Yes, of course. Surely the girl is around here, some place or other."

Jon was beside himself. "I didn't see those things!" he repeated wildly. He threw himself to his knees and crawled back into the cave, but saw no more than he had the first time—sand, gravel, the greenish rock wall and the rotten birch leaves. But now he suddenly remembered that he used to play here as a child—not often, for it was in an out-of-the-way place, but occasionally when they wanted to go on a serious expedition, to expand the borders of their world. And of course that was with Lisa.

"I didn't see those things!" he hollered when he came out again. His head felt as if it had just been clubbed. He wanted to cut it, split it open with a sharp knife so its horrible contents could pour out into the daylight and become clear.

"It doesn't matter," said Kari, taking him by the hand and leading him down the mountain. "Anybody can make a mistake. And it was dark in there."

"No, no. I saw everything else—the stones, the sand . . ."

"Well, okay, but it's nothing to get so upset about . . ."

There was a commotion.

The sheriff was given the clothes, Sakkariassen and other members of Lisa's family identified them, a technical expert from the city examined them and sent them on to Oslo for more thorough examination.

Thirty or forty men with search dogs scoured the ridge and the mountains around the cave, the school children looked on wide-eyed, and the local citizenry searched each other's faces and their memory. It was learned that Lisa's relatives down south hadn't seen her since *before* her last visit to the island—that was in September—but it was not unusual for her to skip her obligatory monthly visit. Her employer had been to her residence a couple of times and, sure enough, had found it empty, but didn't think anything of it. After all, she was known to be unreliable. People wondered why her

125

father hadn't instituted a search for her, but his answer was that he had had absolutely no reason to do so. They had had no regular contact with each other because of their strained relationship. The only contact they did have was mediated by Lisa's oldest sister, and she reported that there were sometimes weeks and even months between letters. Lisa had done strange things all her life. She had run away and created consternation many times, but the concern had always proved to be groundless.

Jon took very little part in all of this. He came home from the mountains in a state of profound disorientation and swallowed a handful of sleeping pills. Elisabeth found him in a coma and sent for the doctor, who rushed over, lifted his eyelids, took his pulse, and removed the rest of the drugs from the medicine cabinet. A day or so later he was conscious again, confused but no longer depressed.

Elisabeth did not reproach him. She fixed the food he wanted, made cocoa, and even put off the packing for a few days to avoid exposing him to any more stress.

When he was healthy again he called up the sheriff and told him bluntly what he had seen in Long Lake. He had already mentioned it to Elisabeth, so now it also had to be reported to the sheriff.

But Long Lake was on the southern part of the island, several miles from the cave on the ridge, and the sheriff had little confidence in Jon and his observations. After all, lots of people wanted to get involved in this affair. Nonetheless, he instituted a search of the lakeshore, engaged a couple of amateur divers, and put in a telephone call to Georg. None of these efforts turned up anything of significance.

"I must say that I'm getting pretty tired of you," he said when Jon called up again to find out how things were going.

"Yeah, I'm sure you are," Jon said.

"Have you had anything at all to do with Lisa recently?"

"No."

"And these nighttime visits to her father?"

"I've told you: it wasn't me."

"And the graffiti on the walls over by the school?"

"No."

He thought he could just as well have answered these questions in the affirmative. What he said didn't seem to make any difference.

"Are you crazy? Obviously the divers haven't found a body or they would have reported it."

"Yeah, I suppose they would."

"And what you may have seen from a distance of four hundred meters, on a gray day, under water—well, one simply can't put any stock in it."

No, he understood. At least he had reported what he thought he had seen.

One evening Karl brought a bottle of whiskey and sat down on the edge of the bed of the sick man.

"I've been doin' a lot of thinkin'," he wheezed. "Tell me: *are* you the one that killed that nutty woman?"

"No."

"She was pretty odd, warn't she?"

"Yeah, I guess you could say that."

"You know that you can say anything to me?"

"Yeah."

"I've known you all yer life. I'm yer neighbor, yer nearest neighbor, don't forget that."

"No."

"Now: *was* it you?"

"No."

"An' all that fuss 'n bother," Karl said, half to himself. "All on account of a nutty broad who maybe ain't even dead. I tol' the wife: Lisa is hidin' out somewhere or other and laughin' at us. That's what I said. She was the kinda woman who liked t' hide 'n laugh at people, warn't she?"

"Yes."

"Yes, and you knew 'er, Jon. Knew 'er real good. That's why I thought you was the one that done it."

This last remark was overheard by Elisabeth, who was busy packing towels in a suitcase in the next room. She came in and gave Karl a piece of her mind. If the old pig thought her brother was a murderer, then *he*—Karl—was ready for the madhouse. And he couldn't excuse himself on grounds that he was drunk, because he was always that way.

Karl had to go.

There was a new storm. This time it came from the northwest, with a lot of heavy snow that gathered in drifts around the houses and flattened out the landscape.

Some of the uproar quieted down. Lisa was not found, either dead or alive. The shocking statement about her was removed from the walls, the examination of the clothing did not reveal anything of a criminal nature, and the investigation conducted by the newspaper was nothing compared to the earlier one that had traced her to Copenhagen. This time there was no social commentary, just a factual report no longer than an obituary notice.

It took only a few days for both journalists and most everybody else to conclude that she was dead. And were it not for that ominous writing on the walls they would have assumed that she had committed suicide or had fallen to her death without anyone else around. People could have made up their minds to wait for a decent period of time—a year, say, which is to say a little longer than the time required by simple considerations of propriety—and then on some ordinary, nondescript Thursday afternoon they could have quietly set up a stone with her name on it in the graveyard by the little gray church, just like they had always done for the fishermen who disappeared at sea. But then there was that painting on the walls. It made people uneasy, and most of them soon divided into two camps: those who thought Lisa had written the message herself

128

before taking her own life, and the more skeptical souls who made much of the fact that they disagreed with the majority and held, rather, that Lisa had been murdered. In the opinion of the latter group, the writing on the wall was the signature of a sick killer. There was also a small third camp consisting of the few people who really *knew* Lisa. They had no opinion on the matter at all. They nodded silently when the issue came up and thought it best to withhold judgment for the time being.

Jon became his normal self once again. Elisabeth went away for a few days to check on the new flat, and he spent the afternoons in a sleeping bag out on the steps, watching heavy, white snowflakes fall from a green winter sky and doing what he could to forget.

Frank came to see him. He said there were tons of codfish in the fjord and wanted Jon to come with him the next morning to set out some lines—*ten* tubfuls. One couldn't handle ten tubfuls alone, it took at least two men, right? No, Jon didn't want to go with him. But Frank kept insisting until Jon said he would go, not because he had any intention of doing it but just so Frank would leave him alone. Frank came back the next day wondering why Jon hadn't met him at the wharf that morning as he had agreed. Jon wondered too. "Yes," he said, shaking his head. "And here we had an agreement and everything." There's nothing to say in a situation like that. Frank just left.

Marta also stopped in to report that Nils hadn't been outside for several weeks, he just sat by the kitchen table and bawled. Jon sent her away. "Let the old devil bawl," he thought out loud after she had left. "I have other things to worry about."

And things didn't get any better when Elisabeth came back, jittery and more uncertain of her decision than ever. The flat was fine, the area was nice, the city was exciting, everything was great. But it was nice here on the island too, she saw that now. Why, she had even gotten a little homesick while she was down there. The tempo of the packing had to be accelerated. Action! And she wanted him to help. In spite of everything, it was his move too.

He gave her a half-hearted yes, but as far as he could see she had already packed most of it, including his things. He had even had to unpack a few small things while she was away—some clean pants, a few kitchen items that he needed for his simple but time-consuming cooking.

He began to hate the place—not only the balls of barbed wire, the junked cars, and the unpainted houses that started to collapse before they were finished, but also the things he normally loved: Nils's stone, where he sometimes sat when the tide was out, the mountain ash in the yard with the heart carved in the bark—which he had looked at every single day since Lisa and he had carved it together once when they were in their puberty. It was wretched here. There was no order. Things were haphazard, out of place. What should he do?

16

He packed.

It was a hard and painful process, contrary to everything he thought and felt and desired. A picture that had hung where it belonged for his entire life—"Grandfather resting"—was torn unceremoniously from the wall and shoved into a box. A jug that his father had gotten in Malaysia, a little flower stand that his mother had polished and painted over and over again in order to make it as pretty as possible, and that she had decorated every Christmas with cotton batting and elves and. . . . One stone was being piled on top of another in a mausoleum that was engulfing his life. He couldn't stand it.

He began to smuggle groceries out of the house: coffee, rye crisp, canned goods, margarine, and other things. He made purchases on his own in addition to the items on the daily lists and carried them down into the old potato cellar while Elisabeth was at school. When she wasn't looking he removed items of clothing from drawers and from boxes that she had already packed—an old windbreaker with a fur collar, mittens that were no longer in use, a scarf, socks, underwear. He packed all of these items into his father's old seaman's bag—old, unimportant things. All the *new* things, including his guns, would be left behind, thus letting Elisabeth know that this time his disappearance could not be explained simply as an ordinary excursion to the mountains. This was to be his last journey—taken in desperation and practically in his stockingfeet—to Long Lake, where he would drown himself.

On the afternoon preceding the day on which Jon intended to carry out his plan, something unexpected happened. Hans's name appeared on the principal's list of teachers for the next year.

"He has deceived me again," said Elisabeth, who didn't even bother to brush the snow off her fur coat before putting it in the closet. "He obviously has not resigned."

She fumed—at herself more than at Hans, for he was just acting as he always did. But this presumably meant that their plans for a tryst that evening were out the window.

"What will you do now?" asked Jon, who had only one thought in his head.

"I don't know. I suppose there's nothing to do."

"Keep nagging him."

"No, I can't bring myself to do that. He just can't stand to leave the children—and I do understand that. But he can't leave that wretched nurse of his either."

She had inadvertently picked up a bear-shaped glass figurine as she was talking, a prize that Jon had won at a shooting contest once. She absentmindedly dropped it into a box containing some protective packing material—one of *her* boxes.

"That's mine," he said automatically.

"Your what?"

"I won it."

She couldn't believe that he would bring up such a thing at a time like this.

"But you *gave* it to me, don't you remember?"

Through the years he had from time to time given her everything he owned—things he didn't care about, even his guns and records. . . . He racked his brain for some way to put the disagreement to rest.

"Jon!" she said suddenly. "Surely you haven't been thinking of doing something stupid?"

It was not the first time she had surprised him with a dangerously accurate premonition, but at the moment she was only thinking of Hans—that her brother might get it into his head to avenge the treachery. He had no trouble at all calming her down.

He put on his coat and went outside. "We need milk," he said—and then took a long detour to stretch out the time. His plan didn't allow for any postponements. The weather forecast was perfect: no more snow, no wind, nondescript weather just like he wanted—a dark and moonless night.

He went home again and said that he had bumped into Hans. "He wants you to meet him. Tonight," he said.

"Oh, really?" she asked suspiciously. "And where is this rendezvous supposed to take place?"

"At Moen."

"Moen?"

She was surprised. "Did he tell you *that*? It's supposed to be a secret."

Jon had known about this secret meeting place for years. He also knew when Hans's wife had night duty at the nursing home.

"You won't be needing it any more from now on," he said gently as he prayed a silent prayer that Hans wouldn't call until nighttime.

"No, I suppose we won't," she said. "Was that all he said?"

"Yes. At the usual time."

He spent the rest of the evening under the covers up in his room. He listened to the weather and to the little sounds Elisabeth made puttering down in the kitchen. He thought he could hear her rehearsing her lines in preparation for the forthcoming meeting with Hans, just like *he* often did when his breast was bursting with righteous indignation. Jon had practically convinced himself that Hans

133

really *was* going to meet Elisabeth at Moen that evening. The man had misled her and hurt her, and he couldn't just sit quietly at home with the kids asleep and his wife at work. No, he had to go out and make amends for his crimes, explain, receive forgiveness. Just so he doesn't call!

He didn't call. And finally Elisabeth left.

Jon got up and put on his clothes, fetched the sack with the food and equipment from the potato cellar, then returned to the house. He stood and looked lovingly at it for several solemn moments before he finally turned and began walking slowly across the heath.

It was milder than had been expected, and a fine mist struck him in the face. The fog clung closely to the ground, creating a moist, impenetrable darkness—but not really as stable a weather situation as he had hoped for. This type of weather never lasted very long, and it was important that his tracks remain visible!

Suddenly he was gripped by a terrible, numbing thought: what if Elisabeth got it into her head *not* to institute a search for him, or at least to postpone it? There were a hundred good reasons for her to do that—an undependable nuisance like him, why should anyone bother searching for the likes of him?

He sank down on a tuft of grass and looked around in desperation. He heard the flapping of wings above his head. The fog banks began to swirl. Suddenly he saw the light in Karl's yard shining like an eye in the darkness.

Jon stood up with renewed determination and walked straight toward the light until he could hear the animals' hooves against the wooden floor. He put down the sack, took his axe and entered the barn. Yellow eyes stared at him through the dank, foul-smelling air. He grabbed the first and best ewe that he could find, dragged her out of the pen and down into the gutter, and struck her on the head again and again until it was totally smashed and the animal was lifeless. He removed two spikes from one of the beams, maneuvered the carcass up onto his shoulders, and nailed the front legs to the wall facing the hay barn. With *one* long cut he slit open the belly so the intestines tumbled out onto the floor. He left the axe lying there, the axe with his initials carved into the handle.

By the time he reached Long Lake, the first snowflakes had already begun to collect like bog cotton on the heather. He found the cove where he had seen the shadow under the divers' boat. That was long ago now, in his former life. He quickly removed his clothes and left them on the ground. He had planned, actually, to keep them on—nobody drowns himself naked—but now the snow would be removing his footprints.

He pulled a big plastic sack over the seaman's bag, held it between his teeth, and began swimming in the ice-cold water. After ten strokes he had lost all contact with his surroundings. He could keep his bearings only by the slight wind that was blowing from the northwest, or by looking back at his own wake. But the lake was very narrow here, no more than a hundred and fifty meters across, so he could manage it.

He kept swimming for a quarter of an hour. He thought about nothing at all. His arms and legs were like iron, and his breath came in short gasps. He was not afraid. He had no concern, either for that which was past or for that which was to come. He felt no sense of loss. He just continued to move his arms and legs. Until the water became a soup of mud, matted roots, and decayed rushes, until his stiff fingers encountered loose sod and clung fast.

He drew a deep breath, rolled the bag laboriously ahead of him, and at last managed with great effort to crawl up onto solid ground. His teeth had cut a hole in the plastic bag, and a little water had leaked in, but most of the contents were still dry. He wiped off his numb body with a handkerchief, put on some dry clothes, and began to walk—with an intense coldness hammering his temples. He reached the cove where the water pipes came down, then continued on up the mountain—stumbling, with one hand on the wooden railing to keep him going in the right direction.

He was on the verge of fainting by the time he got to the little enclosure below the dam. "It's snowing," he thought feverishly as he crawled into hiding and buried himself in the sleeping bag. His hands smelled like lanolin from the wool of the sheep that he had killed. He plunged them into the gravel and scraped them back and forth across the stones until they began to bleed. The odor was in the pores of his skin and under his fingernails; it had burnt itself indelibly into his body; it was like a deep, invisible scar in his skin. He vomited. Water ran out of his eyes, and his breath would not return to normal. It's snowing, he thought despairingly. It's snowing.

17

Two days passed in deep silence as the snow sifted down over the barren landscape. Jon had a fever and cold chills. He saw an eagle lose its grip on the steep mountainside and make a brief flight through the snowy sky. He saw it land and try to get a new grip, saw it take off and make another complete circle, like the last slender hand on the face of a fine clock. He left the sleeping bag only to relieve himself. He slept, let his thoughts wander, and followed the circling of the eagle. Nobody came looking for him.

On the morning of the third day an enormous cloud bank descended upon the sea and the mountains, burying everything in a thick, gray fog. Now his clothes would disappear for good down there on the shore. He saw the eagle take off and land and tried to count how many times it happened. He ate a little and drank coffee that he warmed over the flaming chips of some boards that had once been used as forms for concrete. He was never totally unconscious, but neither was he ever completely clearheaded.

Around noon on the fourth day the wind picked up and began to make a sound like the baying of a pack of dogs. But the endless white expanse remained lifeless as he scanned it with his binoculars. Here and there it was speckled with grayish-black knolls and the dull reflection of small, frozen tarns, and beyond the land lay the iron-gray ocean as far as the eye could see. No color, no movement. And, of course, no dogs.

But the sound came back. It echoed in his ears and stayed there, insistent and real. He kicked the door open and stared out. Nothing. They would never find him. That's how things look on the other side of the ocean, in the empty stare of old Nils, who can't remember anything. It was cold. He didn't know what was real and what wasn't.

The sound did not stop. It was a brook of flowing metal that he had heard all his life—and suddenly he knew: it was a raven! Of course it was a raven. He started to cry. He ate and drank some coffee. His hands no longer smelled of lanolin. The eagle again lost its grip on the mountain. He perceived that it was summer.

The sun shone day and night and the grass grew luxuriously on the meadows. A colorful circle of motor homes and camping trailers filled the soccer field. It was carnival time, with throngs of people, merry-go-rounds, wheels of fortune, lotteries, a roller coaster, men and women in fancy clothes shouting with foreign accents over a static-filled loudspeaker system.

Jon stood at the shooting gallery with the gun held firmly in both hands. He squandered one ten-spot after another, used *two* lousy shots to get his aim right on rifles with crooked barrels. He looted the shelves of the terrified gypsy—took glass figurines and fruit baskets—always with Lisa's happy laughter bubbling like a fountain at his side. She hopped up and down, tugged at his jacket, and clapped her hands.

But Jon got too big for his own good and for his narrow little world. Old Sakkariassen forced his way through the crowd, grabbed his daughter by the arm and dragged her out of the dream right in front of everybody. They were no longer children. The unquestioning freedom of innocence was over. It was in this moment that it happened, this one evening under the glaring lights of the carnival—the watershed, the great divide in Jon's life. He put his hands on the door and pushed. It wouldn't budge.

He was snowed in.

He braced his feet against the pipe and pushed again. The door would not open. Suddenly he was fully alert—not afraid, just remarkably calm.

138

He used his knife to remove the hinges and pulled the door inside. He dug away the snow that tumbled in and kept on digging until the light hit him full in the face.

The fifth day was clear and calm. The winter sun, still hidden from view, created a thin red streak along the southern horizon. All the tarns in the marsh were frozen, as were also many of the coves in Long Lake. Winter was a dazzling white blanket with modest little black houses clustered together to make a village, and from each individual house rose a perpendicular column of smoke.

On the shore of Long Lake stood a tractor, four or five snow scooters, some people, and some dogs. Looking through his binoculars, Jon saw a diver wade out into the water and disappear. He came ashore again with a rope, and the men on shore dragged a dark, formless bundle up into the snow. They wrapped it in something that looked like a blanket and placed it on a platform attached to the tractor.

The diver got a new air tank and waded out again, came up, switched air tanks, and disappeared once more. He continued searching as long as the short day lasted. Jon stood up and wanted to shout, but his legs wouldn't hold his weight. And his voice was husky, inaudible. They did not see him.

The men packed up their equipment and made their way back to the village.

With a piece of wire left over from the cement work, Jon fastened his knife to the two brass valve handles—first one and then the other—and turned off the water.

18

He straightened his back and wiped some drops of moisture off the lens. A raincoat covered the camera to shield it from the wet snow. He was filming Lisa's funeral: some people with bowed heads around a newly dug grave in the churchyard, her elder sister in black, the new minister with hands folded, old Sakkariassen, the cooper in a suit, and some relatives whom Jon did not know.

The casket, covered with a mélange of flowers that contrasted sharply with the gray surroundings, had been placed on the elevator that was to lower it into the grave.

Most of the people in the community had stayed home. Lisa was the daughter of a powerful and unpopular man who had children with the clear intention that they should be boys. She had been odd, and her death had occasioned a lot of nasty rumors. People may have wanted to punish her father, or they may have wanted to spare him; they may have felt guilt, or they may have felt defiance. In any case, they stayed home, and in so doing they contributed— not by design, but with resounding and inadvertent unanimity—to the burial for Lisa that presumably harmonized best with her eccentric life and mysterious death.

The gravedigger sat in a sheltered place near the wall of the church and smoked a cigarette. A gust of wind blew a bouquet of flowers down into the grave. The pastor stopped talking, and Sakkariassen raised his head. He saw Jon over on the mound of dirt, nodded pensively, and began walking toward him. He stopped at a distance of two or three meters and thrust his cane into the snow.

"Won't you ever leave us alone?" he asked.

Ashamed, Jon shrugged his shoulders and averted his eyes.

"I thought you were sick. Somebody said you had pneumonia."

After being found in the mountain by the sheriff's team, Jon had spent four days in bed. He was still exhausted from the fever but was not so bad as to prevent him from standing here and operating a camera.

"So you aren't sick," said the old man. "What is wrong with you, then, that you want to film . . . this?"

"I want to remember it," said Jon.

"Remember? Can't you rather try to forget, like the rest of us? Can't you, just this once, try to be like everyone else? Well?"

Jon averted his eyes again.

"No," he said.

Sakkariassen shook his head slowly, turned around, and, looking glumly at the ground, walked away. Even though the tears on his pale cheeks might have been nothing more than melted snow, Jon felt a momentary lessening of his hatred for Lisa's father. Perhaps Jon *had* had a choice. Perhaps he *could* have done something other than to stand here and take pictures. But he was here. And even though the intensity of the hatred diminished, he felt no regret. He left the camera running.

The mourners waited by the grave, the minister looked up impatiently. Sakkariassen stood motionless.

Seeing the delay, the gravedigger stood up, waved at Jon with a dark-colored crank, and shouted to him to come and help him with one of the straps on the casket elevator. It was twisted, and there was danger that the casket might slip off.

Jon left the camera running, walked over and got down on all fours at the edge of the grave. Spruce twigs had been put in the bottom of the grave to conceal the water, and on top of the spruce needles lay the bouquet that had blown down. Jon tried to read the name of the giver, thinking vaguely that it might be significant, but the ribbon was fluttering and he couldn't read it. For a brief moment he had to close his eyes to fight off a wave of dizziness. Then he lifted the casket and straightened the strap, and the gravedigger was able to insert the crank.

By then Sakkariassen had returned to his place. The minister spoke the final words, nobody cried, and the casket was lowered into the grave.

As those in attendance were leaving the graveyard, Jon took his good time unmounting his camera and tripod. Then he crouched down beside the gravedigger over by the church and waited for a sleet shower to blow over.

The man spit in the snow and said, "Well, I guess there won't be anything else to do here today."

"Won't you be putting the dirt back in the grave?" Jon asked.

"Naw," said the man, spitting again. "This wasn't no ordinary burial. It was just a show for the family. Some guys are comin' to fetch the body—some experts from the city. There's somethin' about it that just ain't right."

Some letters had turned up, sent anonymously to one of the teachers at the school, who had passed them on to the sheriff. They appeared to be Lisa's letters, at least the handwriting was hers. And they sure made for shocking reading, if you could believe those who claimed to know what was in them. It was incredible what that father had done to his daughter through the years. The gravedigger shook his head as if he couldn't believe what he had heard.

"Yeah, I know," Jon mumbled. He, too, had heard about the letters.

"I was told to wait right here. I hafta get a receipt for the body. But you c'n just go."

Jon put the camera and the tripod in a bag, loaded it on his kick sled, and headed back to the village. He didn't like the idea of turning Lisa over to the uncertain fate that now clearly awaited her as the object of a thorough *post mortem* examination. She needed to be left in peace, and he had hoped that they would bury her for good.

A short distance down the road he met two cars. The sheriff was behind the wheel of the first one, and in the passenger seat sat a stranger—a bald, middle-aged man with a shirt and tie under a brown leather jacket. Two dark eyes glanced at him briefly, leaving him with the trembling feeling that he sometimes felt out in the wild when he had to ask a stranger for directions.

The cars turned off the main road and continued on up toward the churchyard.

There was no school because of the funeral, or perhaps because of the tragedy. Nonetheless, Elisabeth was not home. A stranger sat in the kitchen, and he, too, wore a white shirt and tie beneath his outerwear. On the table lay a brown leather case, a scratch pad, and a camera with a flash attachment. The room was quite dark.

Jon turned on a light.

"The door was open," the man said, standing.

"It's always open."

He held out his hand in greeting, but Jon ignored it. He was a small, nervous-looking man whose every movement was quick, furtive. He said he was a journalist from one of the newspapers in Oslo, and he showed Jon an ID card that Jon didn't bother to read. He was here about Lisa.

"You're the one that found her, according to what I've heard. Is that correct?"

Jon thought for a moment. "I didn't see any car," he said, peering out the window.

"Uh . . . no," said the man, smiling from ear to ear. "I came by taxi."

"I didn't see any tire tracks either. You must have been here for some time."

"Hm. Yes, I've been here awhile."

"And nobody was here when you came?"

Uh . . . no."

Jon looked around. Offhand, everything appeared to be in order. He took a turn through the living room and the hall, pulled out a drawer and glanced at the few things that hadn't been packed yet, climbed up to the second floor and inspected his bedroom. Suddenly he began to shiver and had to find an additional sweater. It concerned him that Elisabeth wasn't home. He could think of no natural explanation for her not being at home now.

The journalist had taken a chair.

"Can we sit down?" he said with the same broad smile. "I would like to have a little chat with you."

"Sure, go ahead, sit," Jon said.

But Jon could not sit down. He paced the floor. When he had run away to the mountains, he had left his guns standing in the corner between the refrigerator and the door to the dining room. They were no longer there.

"Did you take my guns?" he asked.

"Your guns? What do you mean?"

"My *guns!*" he bellowed. "Somebody warned you. Is that why you hid them?"

The journalist insisted that he didn't know what Jon was talking about. He was formal and condescending, as if he were accustomed to denying absurd accusations. There was something about him that Jon found exceptionally irritating. Maybe it was his smile, that presumably was supposed to be convincing but was absolutely vacuous. Jon reached into the top drawer of the cupboard and took out the bread knife.

"If you don't tell me where my guns are," he said, grabbing the man by the neck, "I'm going to cut out one of your eyes! That one!" He pointed the sharp blade at the journalist's right eye. The man stiffened instantly, and the smile disappeared. His expression

144

changed to fear as he stared at the tip of the knife blade quivering menacingly less than an inch from his eye.

"I haven't taken them," he said breathlessly. "I don't have any idea what you're talking about."

Jon looked at him carefully. Then he released his grip, put the knife back in the drawer, and sat down wearily in a chair. "People don't tell the truth when they have the upper hand," he said. "Only when they are afraid. It must have been Elisabeth, then."

"Elisabeth?" stammered the journalist as he labored to regain his composure. He rubbed his neck and groaned. His scratch pad and pen and the contents of his equipment bag were strewn all over the floor, but he made no effort to pick them up.

"My sister," Jon said. "Have you seen her?"

"I told you I haven't seen anyone! There was nobody here when I came, not a soul. I just came to have a chat . . ."

Jon couldn't just sit there. He took the basket from the top of the refrigerator, emptied its contents on the table, and rifled feverishly through it. He checked the notebook and the scratch pad by the telephone stand, searched everywhere he could think of where she might have left a message for him. Through the window he saw two headlights coming up the hill a short distance away. They disappeared into the hollow, then reappeared in the yard, pointing his way, illuminating the blowing snow.

"Come in!" he said aloud when he heard a knock. He was almost relieved. The sheriff and the stranger entered the room.

A deep wrinkle extended from ear to ear above the stranger's dark eyes, and now Jon could see that the eyes were not threatening. They expressed neither friendliness nor hostility; they were neutral at all times.

Jon sat down. That stupid journalist was no longer of any interest to him. Elisabeth's absence had also faded into insignificance. If there had been any sense of direction in what he had been doing these past months, it was there no longer. This was the moment toward which he had been moving—not to lay down his burden, but to start his real work.

The man was from the criminal police department in Oslo. His name was Hermansen.

"Hello," said Jon.

"I would like to have you come with me to the city," he said, "so we can talk together at the hotel there."

"Can't we do that here?" Jon asked.

"Is this an arrest?" the journalist wanted to know. He had to show his ID again, and Hermansen—in contrast to Jon—showed considerable interest in it. He kept it, and made much of the fact that the newspaperman had gotten here so quickly. How did this happen? The journalist said he had received a tip from a colleague, but he didn't give many details. "One hears rumors about a place like this," he informed them.

But the policeman would not be put off by folklore. He wanted the facts: his source, the details of the rumors he had heard, and everything the man might know or think about the matter at hand. It was obvious that it was Marit who had sent him.

"Did you come on foot?" asked Hermansen. "I didn't see any car." There was a little levity, but it was strained.

Throughout this time the sheriff had remained standing by the door with his arms crossed. When Hermansen was finished, he said that the journalist could call a taxi from a nearby telephone.

"What about that one?" He nodded toward the telephone. "It's just a few hundred meters up the road," said Hermansen.

"Elisabeth has already been informed," said Hermansen when they were alone. Jon had to find a bag. It was already packed. It was really intended for use during the move: all it needed was a toothbrush and it was ready to go.

The policeman looked around the barren home as Jon performed his usual ritual—emptied the ashes onto the compost heap behind the house, threw three shovelfuls of coal into the stove, and opened the draft. When the fire was burning he closed the damper almost all the way, made sure that the burners on the stove were turned off, and clicked off the ceiling light. He put on the jacket that he had bought in Copenhagen.

"Are you going to be moving?"

He nodded.

"What's wrong with that picture over there—since it isn't going with the other stuff?"

It was a drawing that hung over the sink. Jon's drawing, a poorly executed sketch that he had once made for Lisa. He had never given it to her, but Elisabeth thought it was "cute"—which is what she usually thought about the more conciliatory aspects of Jon's personality. It was summertime in the picture—summer as depicted in the dry, pale hues of a paintbox.

"Do you mind if I take it along?"

"No."

"It's very good."

He rolled it up carefully, and Jon pretended that he hadn't heard what the man said.

The sheriff got out at the civic center, and Jon and Hermansen drove on in the policeman's car toward the ferry landing on the inner side of the island—about a twenty-minute drive on the slippery winter roads. Hermansen wanted to keep up a conversation, remarking several times that the scenery on the island was very pretty.

"I've never been this far north before. It must be sad to be moving."

"Yes."

"What kind of work do you do?"

"Nothing much."

He wanted to know who lived on the various farms, whether Jon had been up to the highest mountain peaks. He asked about hunting

147

and fishing opportunities, confiding that he himself was an avid hunter. He also wanted detailed information about the water project, and he refused to be put off by Jon's reluctant monosyllables. He repeated his simple questions in the same conversational tone until it was impossible not to answer them. Eventually he let it be known that he had something in mind in addition to all this chit-chat.

"Do you know why I am here?" he asked.

"Yes," said Jon. "To ask whether I killed Lisa."

They were on a straight stretch of road at that point, and the policeman could take his eyes off the road. He looked at Jon.

"Well, *did* you kill her?" he asked.

"No."

"But you know who did?"

"Yes. Her father."

But this answer didn't satisfy anybody. A father does not kill his own daughter. In a policeman's psychological understanding, and in Jon's hate-filled insanity, perhaps he can be imagined to prepare the way—to arrange the mental circumstances, so to speak—but he does not kill her. He can kill his parents, his son, his wife—and they him—but never a daughter; she alone is inviolable.

Jon now realized this truth in all its horror. He had seen Sakkariassen's tear-stained cheeks up there in the churchyard—if, indeed, it was tears that he had seen. He was crying for having prepared the way, for one does not kill a daughter. One does all kinds of other things to her, but one does not kill her! Sakkariassen was no different from anyone else. He wanted sons. He was normal.

"Maybe nobody killed her," Jon mumbled.

"Maybe," said the policeman, "but we have every reason to assume that someone did."

"Who could have any reason to kill someone like Lisa?"

"I don't know. I never met her."

They coasted down through the sharp curves leading to the ferry landing, and Jon thought that maybe Elisabeth had gone to the city. In that case she would be coming back on this ferry. Then he remembered her face peering down at him during his recent illness. She had been suspiciously quiet, had withheld her reproaches, had not said a word about either the phony tryst he had sent her to or the sheep that he had slaughtered in such a macabre way. She was endowed with the patience of a seasoned human being who knew that her burdens were about to grow lighter.

When the ferry arrived and the passengers began streaming out along the gangway, he scanned their faces but did not really expect to see her.

"Are you expecting someone?" Hermansen asked.

Elisabeth was not there.

"No," he said. And they drove aboard the ferry.

19

From the hotel room they could see the harbor and the city. That which in his father's day had been nothing but a collection of docks and bridges supported by poles had by Jon's day been transformed into a Klondike of solid concrete, gas stations, and wide streets swarming with motorcycles and cruising Americans— all the result of the profits from the fishing industry. New houses were being built at a hectic pace, and the harbor was lined with a row of newly constructed fish processing plants. The oil business, too, had produced enormous changes—new people, a new hospital, still more houses, a helicopter base, and the most curious specialized businesses.

So when Hermansen devoted his attention to his papers for a few minutes and Jon stopped trying to think, he looked out on a modern coastal city that was approaching Christmas. It snowed every day. The delivery boats serving the area transported tons of Christmas trees and beer, and the people who lived on the nearby islands came to the city to do their Christmas shopping. Under the glare of huge overhead lights, the fishing boats were being steam-cleaned and their keels covered with grease to protect them through the winter season. By the breakwater stood an oil rig awaiting final preparation, and in the background, barely visible in the faint light of a winter day in northern Norway, loomed the blue mountains of Jon's island.

"Where were you born?" Hermansen asked for about the sixth time, for since the first moment they had met Jon had been unresponsive to questions about his personal affairs. He had been relieved when he was taken into custody. It was like a release, the firing of a weapon that finally went off after an inordinately long delay.

"It's written right there," he said, pointing to a sheet of paper.

"I know that, but I want to hear you say it. I want to get you talking. You hardly say a word. It says here that you were born at home."

"Hm."

"Was that common in this area at that time?"

"I don't know."

Then they continued with when he was baptized, when he started school, his confirmation, his parents' birth dates, occupations, and deaths, Elisabeth and the chaotic course of her life.

There was little or no conversation about Lisa. When he had no more questions about Jon and his family, Hermansen got him to concentrate on the island and the conditions there. And even though Jon didn't fully understand what this had to do with the matter at hand, he often did his best to dredge up rumors and anecdotes, including some that one would normally tell only in wartime or if one were drunk.

"So you think the grass fire that spread to the fish works on North Island was deliberately set?"

Jon had not said that, at least not in so many words.

"Do you think Sakkariassen set it himself?"

It had happened so long ago, he couldn't remember it very clearly.

"But why would he do something like that?"

"Oh, I suppose it was too big," said Jon.

"Too big?"

"Sure. He had two separate operations, with too many expensive machines. And there weren't many fish."

"Hm. Are you sure that he was the one who did it?"

"No."

From time to time Hermansen made a point of being unpredictable. In the middle of a hunting story, for example—one of the few times that Jon really went into considerable detail—he suddenly broke in and asked him if he played an instrument of any kind.

"No," Jon said tersely, deflated by the interruption.

"But you like music?"

"Yes."

"I noticed your records. We could have them brought here. I'm sure we could borrow a stereo."

Shortly thereafter, Jon wanted to shed some light on the reason for the wretched conditions on Karl's farm.

"He drinks," said Jon. It was generally agreed that there was a connection between Karl's drinking and the fact that he had been on the verge of bankruptcy his whole life—*apparently* so, in any case, for the man was something of a mystery.

Rimstad came up in the discussion, as an engineer and as Jon's employer, also the divers, Lisa's siblings, Sakkariassen, and Hans and the water project. Jon began to get tired of all this preoccupation with trivialities. He couldn't care less, for example, about how long Erik—the sheriff—had known Elisabeth. Yes, they were in the same class in school, but he didn't know if Erik knew who had set the fire. But everyone else sure did.

"And still it was not reported?"

"No."

"It was also in the newspaper."

"Yes."

"I have the article right here. Funny business, this—as usual. Couldn't it have been someone else, or an accident?"

"No."

They talked about the fishing, and about the various kinds of work Jon had done through the years.

"Why did you quit the fishing job?"

"Oh, I dunno."

"Didn't you like it?"

152

"No."

"You were at the fish works, but quit there too?"

Yes, Jon thought one shouldn't do too much of something one didn't like. Elisabeth and Hans had done that, and they didn't amount to anything either, so you might as well indulge in the things you enjoy.

"*They didn't amount to anything either?* But they're teachers! They have an important civic responsibility to fulfill."

"Hm."

"What kind of a mentality is *that?*"

Jon hadn't given much thought to what kind of a mentality he had, nor had he considered what the alternatives might be. Things were just fine with him.

"Fine!?"

"Yeah. . . . Fine."

"You didn't take military training either. To go on disability—is that anything for a strong, young man like you to do? And you're not downright stupid, are you?"

Jon laughed out loud.

They talked about still other people, about the whole island.

"I need to understand how this place thinks," said Hermansen. "And these divers. That's quite a story you claim they are hiding: they're supposed to have found a body and dumped it back in the lake?"

"A shadow. All I saw was a shadow."

"But Lisa was found right where you saw the shadow, so one can't help but ask why they did it."

"I suppose they were afraid."

"If they had something to hide, yes. Otherwise, not."

Jon wasn't so sure. He had been afraid all his life, and that didn't mean that he had a murder on his conscience.

"But would that have kept you from reporting something like that?"

153

"Maybe."

"Yes," Hermansen said with a smile. "As a matter of fact, you saw the shadow without reporting it."

"I did report it. To Elisabeth and the sheriff. But nobody takes me seriously."

"Poor fellow. It was you that wrote on the walls too, wasn't it?"

Jon hesitated for a moment. "Yes," he said.

"It was what might be called a major defensive maneuver, wasn't it?"

Jon didn't know what Hermansen was talking about.

Thus it went for two days. Hermansen read papers, pile after pile, asked questions, was alternately stupid and intelligent. They ate in the room or down in the restaurant, people came and talked with them, the telephone rang; Hermansen sometimes disappeared for several hours at a time, then returned with more papers, more questions, more trivialities.

And Jon stared out the window, looked at the harbor and the boats, at busy people hurrying to and fro in the pre-Christmas rush—and at the blue island that seemed to sink deeper and deeper into the sea.

On the third evening Hermansen decided that the game was over. The news had just concluded on TV, a maid who was making up the beds was asked to leave, and Jon had to sit still. Stop rubbing your hand through your hair, he told himself; being nervous isn't going to help.

"We're going to pull together the loose ends," said Hermansen.

If the man had been unpredictable before, he now became absolutely impossible. "We'll start with your account of things," he said. "That gives us two possibilities. Either the divers have killed her, or else they have done something else that they want to hide—presumably something in connection with Lisa . . ."

"What do you mean?"

154

"You know that as well as I."

"No."

"Let's leave that for now, if it's unpleasant for you. Okay?"

Jon was on the verge of saying yes.

"You liked Lisa, didn't you?"

"Yes."

"Why did you say yesterday that you don't remember Elisabeth's birth date?"

"I had forgotten it."

"Forgot when your own sister was born? You gave her a present on her last birthday."

"Hm."

"Do you remember what you gave her?"

"I forget a lot."

"How can you know that?"

The questions were asked in a staccato tempo, and Jon had a lot of trouble following along. He tried to focus his thoughts, couldn't think of any answer, and just repeated that he forgot a lot.

Hermansen held a sheet of paper in front of his eyes, and Jon saw the official stamp of the municipality under Rimstad's signature.

"The divers have been here before," he said. "It was the same firm that put in the old water pipe twelve years ago. They've sent people here several times during the intervening years—including Georg at least once—for maintenance and repairs. Service was part of the original contract, and in time it got to be quite extensive. *That* pipe, too, was obviously a mistake. The question is whether that explains in any way why the divers were *afraid*. It also appears that Rimstad and Georg didn't get along very well. Do you know why?"

"No."

"There's not very much about the people on this island that you don't know, Jon!"

He gave no reply.

"Well?"

155

No, he didn't know.

"Lisa disappeared on August 27—*presumably*—and it says here"—he read from another piece of paper—"new charting of the bottom of Long Lake in connection with the proposed aqueduct." The work was carried out by Georg and his partner between the 25th and the 30th of August. That means that all the equipment, the boat and everything, was already at the lake when she disappeared, three weeks before you saw the shadow. They could sink her without being seen."

"Yes."

"I mean, one would need a boat for that."

"Yes."

"Or somebody else could have done it while they were in town getting drunk—as a matter of fact, anybody who knew the divers' routines. They did a lot of drinking on weekends, didn't they?"

"Yes."

"The 27th was a Saturday." He referred to another sheet of paper, a calendar, and the Youth Association's program of activities for the fall season. "There was a party at the community center, and they were there."

"Oh?"

"Were *you* there?"

He didn't remember. Maybe. He went to most of the parties. At least he was in the area, hidden some place or other in the woods nearby.

"As far as I have been able to determine, you were *not* there," said Hermansen.

"Well, maybe I wasn't, then."

"Lisa was there, however. Several people saw her with the divers, especially this Georg. He evidently is something of a Casanova. There were quite a few of the men on the island, in addition to Rimstad, who didn't especially like him. Do *you* like him?"

"I don't know."

"You don't have any reason to, do you?"

156

He rubbed his hand through his hair and looked at the floor. "Maybe not," he said.

"You and Karl were at his house drinking that evening. You were mad. Do you remember that?"

"No."

"*He* remembers it because the two of you began to quarrel about getting paid for rounding up sheep, something you never had asked for previously. You and he eventually got in a fight, and he had to throw you out." Jon smiled.

"Don't smile, Jon. That drunkard is of no more help to you than he is to me."

Silence.

Then followed a veritable bombardment of facts: the divers' final report, equipment and transport lists—including mention of a lost compressor—maps and charts with alternatives 1, 2, 3, etc., as well as expense estimates, medical records, an autopsy report, airplane and ferry tickets, weather reports, several of Jon's personal belongings, drawings, some letters he could only vaguely remember, Christmas cards, report cards from school, receipts for medicine— they must have turned the house upside down—where was Elisabeth?—newspaper clippings, bus schedules, photographs, a report of an examination that he had been compelled to undergo (at Elisabeth's insistence) during puberty after smashing some furniture because he hadn't been allowed to have guns in the house—an endless procession of heartless, trivial facts. Hermansen nailed it all down—one person, one day, one act after another—placing each detail in exactly the right place in an irrefutable pattern of life on the island. The truth, as he called it, the naked truth.

Jon was groggy. He was out of his element. He answered and reacted as best he could, but all the time his ears kept ringing with the warning: *there's always some hidden motive.* It was like acrophobia, as if a cloud layer suddenly blew away revealing with photographic clarity the rock-covered slope of an abyss at the very spot where he had felt that he was on solid ground. When he began to fall, he just

157

let it happen, relieved to be getting away—to the island, to the shimmering pictures of summer with the living Lisa.

Hermansen offered him some black coffee. It was late at night. "The rest is free invention," he said. They had gone through every single day since the 27th of August insofar as there were any references to those days in Hermansen's papers. "You're good at making stuff up, Jon. Now it's your turn."

Jon said nothing.

"There is one other man in this story. Hans. You and Lisa were in his class during the first years that he was a teacher here. Now he sleeps with Elisabeth. Who else?"

Jon didn't answer.

The policeman shoved two photographs across the table, but as far as Jon was concerned it could just as well have been two pieces of brown paper. He was far away.

"Lisa and Elisabeth. They look alike, have you noticed? Of course you have. But the similarity is only esthetic. What kind of a relationship was there between Hans and Lisa?"

"Relationship?"

"You heard what I said."

"I don't know."

"People on the island say that it was because of *him* that she had to leave."

"I don't know."

"That's just a rumor?"

"Yes."

"One that *you* have never heard?"

"No."

"When I look for a motive, I always start with the most banal candidate. I listen to the dirtiest hint that I can dredge up from my imagination—for one does not commit crimes out of ecstasy. And the first thing I wanted to know was whether she was pregnant. She

158

wasn't when she was found—but she was when she left the island about two and a half years ago.

The white fingers held up another piece of paper. "She had an abortion." He gave the name of a hospital and a doctor, also the date and the year that the procedure was performed. "Presumably on her father's initiative, although he insists that he knew nothing about it. What is it that makes a father pressure a disturbed daughter to endure such a Medieval ritual—an abortion and banishment from her home?"

Jon didn't know.

"I would bet that there was something abhorrent about the pregnancy. Incest? Idiocy? Was it her teacher? Was it you?"

He let Jon think about these hammer blows for awhile before continuing in a lower voice: "Does the pregnancy have anything at all to do with the murder? My dirty imagination wants to exclude the diver, but common sense drags him back in. . . . Do you think this is pretty rough, Jon?"

"No."

"It gets rougher."

"Hm."

"But no doubt this is old hat to you. This is how life looks to you, isn't it?"

"No."

"Witnesses report that on Saturday, the 27th of August, sometime between eleven and twelve in the evening, there was an argument at the community center between Lisa and Georg. She left in a huff, and nobody tried to stop her or talk to her, as that apparently was fairly normal behavior for her. Nobody—not even the divers—remembers what the argument was about. That was the last time she was seen alive . . ."

Jon hadn't heard the last few sentences. He was on his way around the table to defend his lifestyle. It *didn't* look like Hermansen said. It was a *good* life. He grabbed his tormentor around the throat, but Hermansen must have been expecting it because he fended him off with a well-aimed blow, slapped him in the face a couple of times, and maneuvered him back to the chair.

"You're losing consciousness, Jon!" he shouted in the same machinegun-like tone of voice he had used earlier. "And when that happens, you don't know what you are doing, do you?"

"No!"

"*When* do you lose consciousness, Jon? No, look at me and listen when I talk to you. You've slept long enough now. You lose consciousness when something irritates you, isn't that right? But what is it that irritates you? Can you tell me that?"

"Stop."

"Answer me, then! You're not the one who is dead, Jon. It's Lisa." He shouted: "*It's Lisa! Listen to me!*"

"Yes, yes, I'm listening! Stop!"

"But do you *understand* it!? Do you *understand* it!?"

"Yes, yes, yes!"

There was a long silence. Hermansen sat down again.

"You're a smart devil," he said. "A pipsqueak and a fool, but smart as a whip. Do you hear me?"

Jon did not answer.

"Do you hear me?" the policeman shouted again.

"Yes, yes."

"You sank the compressor in the marsh in order to get them to search where you thought you had seen the body. You turned off the water so they could find you. You frightened Sakkariassen at night and sent the divers your own cat in brine to get them to react and reveal how much they knew. How did they react?"

"Sakkariassen reported me. Georg didn't react at all."

"And that confused you?"

"Yes."

"Why?"

Jon was beginning to come around again. He had never really thought that Georg could kill anyone. The diver was in the picture

160

only because Jon didn't know how much he knew. But of course it was doubtful that there was anything to be gained by repeating this to Hermansen. He just said he didn't know why.

"Sakkariassen or the diver?" bellowed the policeman.

Jon thought that Sakkariassen best suited his purpose. It was around him, the man who had ruined life for him and Lisa, that the laborious network had been spun. But now he didn't fit in the story, not at all.

"Jon, do you have something to tell me," Hermansen asked impatiently, "or don't you?"

"I don't," said Jon. "I don't remember."

He started to cry.

20

They were out on the island.

Hermansen had been there before, had seen the places and talked with the people. Now he wanted Jon to point things out, to investigate with him, and he displayed the same curiosity out in the open as he had amidst the piles of paper in the makeshift office. They climbed up on the ridge and looked under the stone where Lisa's clothing had been found. They visited the empty house. They sat for a time in Karl's kitchen and drank thin coffee. Rimstad took them out to Long Lake on a snowmobile so they could walk around on the ice and talk about the divers' work, look at the mountains and the reservoir through the binoculars, and recount what had happened one more time.

When they came to the fish works on North Island, Hermansen went in by himself.

It was cold, darkness was falling, and the snow clung like fine dust to the car windows. Jon listened to the radio as he was waiting, and thought about Elisabeth. He had gotten a telephone number but hadn't tried it yet. She had run away to escape the sight of the tragedy. Nobody believed him any more. Karl wouldn't even look him in the eye, and it was not because of the sheep. Margrete had quickly poured coffee and then fled teary-eyed into the next room. Rimstad had smirked, whereas in the past there had never been a sign of such a thing on the engineer's honest face. And Hermansen? He had gotten a medical confirmation of Jon's poor memory, but he doubted the validity of the entry in the medical record, which had been written by a medical student who happened to be there on rotation. He talked with the fellow by telephone and learned that he had just written down Jon's own statements. "One should be able to rely to some extent on the patient," he had said. He had called Jon depressive because that is what he was, and he had prescribed Valium because the district medical director at that time was passing it out to practically everybody in the area.

"If you can lie to me you can lie to a doctor," was Hermansen's terse comment.

So why did he let him sit here alone and unguarded? Jon couldn't understand it.

"It's Christmas everywhere," he said when he came back. "Tons of food and decorations. But it smells rotten anyway."

The policeman had dropped some of the formalities. His necktie was back at the hotel, he was unshaven, and he had donned a parka and hiking boots. "Quite a chap, old Sakkariassen, eh? The one daughter takes care of the house, doesn't she?"

"Yes."

"I wonder how she can stand it. I want to see the fish works. Is that it down there?"

"Yes," said Jon, "but it's against the law to go in there."

"We *are* the law, Jon, have you forgotten? Come on."

"No," he said. "I don't want to."

Hermansen had already gotten out of the car, but he got back in. "Now you are making me curious," he said antagonistically. "What is it that you don't want me to see?"

Jon couldn't tell him that he just didn't want some clumsy cop tramping around there in his hallowed past. He remained silent.

They waded down through knee-deep snow. It hadn't been shovelled here for days, boats and docks lay buried in snow along the dark green surface of the sea. The door to the salting building was locked, but Jon was able to open it with a knife blade. He followed Hermansen through the cleaning shed and up to the cooper's shop, through the smells and the memories, until they stood at the opening on the south side and looked out.

"It's a pretty sight," said Hermansen.

Under the snow lay equipment that was no longer in use—barrels, rusty tubs, and stacks of wooden poles, cleaning benches, and floats. The breakwater and the flat, white islands stood out in contrast to the black ice floes in the sea. The clouds, high in the sky, seemed as near as the scenery in a theater, and together with the gently falling snow they formed the walls of a huge glass tower. A flock of eider ducks flew slowly away.

"They don't even have a proper picture of her," said Hermansen. "Can you understand that?"

"They do have pictures. They just didn't show them to you."

"Nonetheless. It seems as if they didn't really want to see her when she was alive, and now they want more than anything to forget her. I always manage to form some kind of picture of the victim, but this time I've found it unusually difficult."

Jon didn't like these poetic digressions, he didn't like the policeman's low, unctuous voice, and he didn't like the look of his brown eyes gazing off into the distance like tourists do when they are discussing the general fate of humankind. He didn't like being here.

"It's cold," he said, shaking his shoulders. "Shall we go?"

"No, no, we're not going yet."

Hermansen took plenty of time. "That opening there, what is it for?"

The small opening in the dormer on the landward side used to accommodate the cables from a winch used to pull the fish wagons up to the drying racks. Hermansen lifted the latch and opened the door.

"This must be the perfect hiding place," he said. "This was where you and Lisa spied on her father, wasn't it?"

Jon had forgotten that little opening. He pushed the policeman aside and saw that he could look right into the farmhouse up on the hill. You could see a Christmas tree behind the curtains, and some shadowy figures who walked here and there and were busy. On the second floor, you could even make out the pattern of the wallpaper. He recognized it as Lisa's room when she was a child.

"Who is the old man?" Hermansen asked, standing beside him.

"The cooper."

The old man pulled a fish case into the hallway and closed the door behind him as Jon leafed through one difficult layer of memories after another.

"You've never been especially talkative, Jon, but today you are more than quiet. What's bothering you?"

"Nothing."

"You're in a daze. Tell me about this loft. Tell me what the various pieces of equipment are used for. How about that knife there, for example?"

"It's a scaling knife."

"And this thing here?"

"A net buoy. In the old days they used barrels as buoys."

But he remained as distant as before. Now Lisa got up from the sofa there in her room and gave a sign meaning, "I can't come."

"Let's go outside," said Hermansen.

They went down the stairs and out onto the snow-covered wharf.

"That fish farm over there—that's Sakkariassen's too, I suppose?"

"No, he doesn't like that sort of thing. It's run by a couple of young fellows."

"How long ago was it that you were here, Jon?"

"A month . . . two months."

"Before that?"

"Two and a half years."

"When Lisa left the island, right?"

He nodded.

The policeman dropped that sensitive topic and began talking about the fish business and everyday life. Jon talked reluctantly about seining and salting processes, proprietary spice mixtures, lumpfish, and dried codfish with their bellies turned eastward. They talked a bit about weather and boats, about harbor conditions and life on the sea, and eventually they returned to the second floor of the salting building.

"What were you wearing the last time you saw Lisa?"

He didn't remember when he last saw Lisa—in the version of events that he had given the policeman. He said he didn't know.

"Some of your clothes are missing, including a sweater that Elisabeth described as your favorite garment. You wore it all the time, summer and winter. Until it disappeared. Do you know which one I mean?"

He remembered the sweater. It was old, ragged, worn out. "I threw it away," he said.

The policeman nodded.

"When you last saw Lisa, was she wearing the clothes that you and the others found under the stone while you were rounding up sheep? A green coat with a high collar, a gray sweater, a woolen scarf with blue and black stripes that she had knitted herself, kerchief, handbag, pants with a hole in the left knee . . .

"I don't remember when I last saw her," he said testily.

"That's how she was dressed at the party, that Saturday."

"Hm."

"But not when she was found. Then she was wearing one of Georg's coveralls—and your old sweater. Do you have any explanation for that?"

"No."

"Why didn't she want to go south again?"

Jon turned around and looked intently at him, as if he had suddenly awakened.

166

"What do you know about that?" he asked. This was something that Hermansen absolutely *couldn't* know anything about.

"It's not so difficult to guess that she was homesick. That happens to everybody. But what did she have to come home to? You?"

No answer.

"*Only* you?"

Still no answer.

"You can just as well answer me, Jon. After me there will be others. It will go on and on."

"Let them come. I haven't done anything."

"Did you see much of her the last time she was home?"

"I already told you—*I don't remember!*"

"Her father refused to let her see you then, too, didn't he?"

"Yes!" he shouted. Then, more calmly: "Yes."

"Did you think about her a lot when she was away?"

"Constantly!" Calmly again: "Every day. I saw her. Always. I talked with her. Every day. Is that what you want to hear?"

Hermansen flung the scaling knife forcefully against the wall, and for a long time neither of them said anything. It seemed to Jon that even the light and the smells ceased, and it occurred to him that the policeman's smile harbored many good reasons for him to be afraid.

"You're smart," said Hermansen. "Nobody knows Lisa. But nobody really knows you either, isn't that right?"

A door slammed, breaking the silence. Jon opened the window and saw Sakkariassen come out in the yard with a snow shovel in his hands. He started shovelling a path—slowly, haltingly, like a stammering child who is being made to read aloud from an incomprehensible book. He had used his last ounce of strength to get fresh water to the fish works, more water than he could ever need. That done, he had lost interest in both the water and the fish works. He was winding down, like Nils. Old age made him pitiable and poor. It brought forgiveness. "He's shovelling snow," Jon thought to him-

167

self—a shovelful here, a shovelful there, with no system, no rhythm, no strength. It was a bewildering sight that undermined all his efforts to make things fit into a just pattern. Life is not fair. It begins, one keeps it going for awhile, and it ends—both for human beings and for sea gulls.

When he closed his eyes he could see the marshes to the south near Long Lake—in sparkling summer light, with the pollen glowing silently in the heather, and the wild mountains where the snow never *totally* disappeared. His land. The very thought of it created a peace and a sturdy confidence that no one could destroy.

He opened his eyes again and saw Hermansen. For the first time he asked a question on his own initiative. He wanted to know how Sakkariassen had reacted to his visit, what he had said.

"Not much," said the policeman, somewhat reluctantly. He was standing very close to Jon, and, like him, saw the shovelled pathway nearing the gateposts by the farmhouse. "But no doubt I left too soon."

"How so?"

"In my business one isn't always sociable. It's only when people start to feel uncomfortable that one learns anything. Sometimes it's hard to hang in there until one learns something."

"Yes," said Jon.

"Do you know what I'm talking about?"

The policeman was so close that Jon could feel his breath on his ear. For a moment he had the impression that it was not just *he* who had been observing but that someone had also been observing *him* during the past few months.

"Was it you who sent those letters to the teacher?" asked Hermansen.

"No."

"There are no fingerprints on them, and the salutation has been clipped off. Nonetheless, it's obvious that they were written to you. Thus the only person who could have sent them, other than you, is Elisabeth, and she hasn't even seen them."

"She's lying."

Elisabeth again. That made the story about the letters more idiotic than this stranger could understand.

"About what? Do you think that she is the one who sent the letters, or that . . . ?"

"I don't think anything. They're not my letters."

"Some letters were also found in Lisa's room, including some from you—but none that fit in with these particular ones. Doesn't that strike you as strange?"

Jon had no opinion about that.

"We have reason to believe that those letters have been removed," Hermansen continued. "Have you been away from the island any time recently?"

"No."

"How about the trip to Copenhagen?"

"Oh, yes, I was there."

"What did you do there?"

Jon didn't know what he had done there. He just *was* there. He rarely knew why he did anything. He just did what he *had* to do, went where his life led him, just as water runs where it runs.

"I went there looking for Lisa," he said.

"Even though you knew that she wasn't there?"

"I didn't know that she wasn't there."

"What she writes about her father is pretty gross. Did she correspond with anyone here on the island other than you?"

"I don't know."

Hermansen smiled again.

On the way back Hermansen stopped in the pass high in the mountains and ordered Jon out of the car. In the trunk he had a rifle in a padded leather case, an expensive precision weapon the likes of which Jon had never seen, not even in his brochures.

He was allowed to assemble the rifle and hold it reverently in his hands. Hermansen opened a steel box containing ammunition,

169

took out a frame with targets, and in the waning moments of the blue winter day they lay in the snow drifts and took turns shooting.

"You're a helluva marksman," he said. And that was all he said, for he offered no explanation for this intermezzo. It was like a pause in the midst of serious business, a momentary respite. Jon, in any case, could see no connection. If there were one, it must be that Hermansen wanted to see him shoot. And perhaps he did give an explanation of sorts, for as they were packing the rifle away Hermansen nodded thoughtfully and said, almost to himself, that he had noticed the new wall on Jon's house. "You *can* do some things, Jon," he said. "And that doesn't totally fit the picture, does it?" But Jon said he *couldn't* do anything. Yes, he could shoot, and he could do a little carpentry, but that was all.

A snowplow came by followed by a string of cars, and Hermansen fell in line at the end of the convoy. It was snowing hard now, but after they had passed an alder grove and descended to the flat land on the inner side of the island it let up. A man in orange coveralls stopped them and said they had to wait because a bus was stuck in the curve just ahead. Hermansen chuckled and said the situation reminded him of Canada, where he had spent several years during his youth.

"What if the snowplow hadn't happened to come by just now?"

Jon was about to say that on his island the snowplows didn't just *happen* to come by—they timed their trips to coincide with the ferry departures whenever possible—but suddenly he recognized the people in the car in front of them. It was Hans, and beside him sat Marit, the journalist. Hermansen saw them as well. He just nodded and tapped his fingers on the steering wheel.

"She plans to write an article about this water affair," he said. "The municipality is bankrupt and wants to adopt a budget that is in deficit."

Then, coaxed along by Hermansen's good humor, Jon posed his second question of the day: "Do you think he might have done it?"

170

Hermansen smiled even more broadly.

"He is a man with ideas," he said. "He came here ten years ago to bring them to reality. One can do strange things in such a situation. What do *you* think?"

"Lisa wanted money," he said.

"What for?"

"She wanted to go and get her things, in order to move back. But her father wouldn't give her a nickel. That's why she went to Hans."

"When? The same day she disappeared?"

"Yes."

"Are you sure?"

"Uh . . . no."

"But *that* she went to Hans to ask for money—are you sure of that?"

"Yes."

Hermansen looked straight ahead and said, "Obviously, Hans didn't give her anything either. Therefore she went to the divers at the party—to Georg, with whom she also had had a relationship. That's what they were quarreling about. Is that what you think?"

"Yes."

"This isn't just something you are sitting here and making up?"

"No."

"And why has nobody told me this before?"

Jon had no explanation for this, nor did Hermansen expect one from him. He was already out in the swirling snow, by the car in front, where he pounded on the window and talked to Hans. They talked for four or five minutes, and Marit also said a few words. His face was red when he came back.

"Let me think a bit out loud for you, Jon," he said. "The method by which Lisa was killed doesn't really tell us much about the murderer. She was beaten with a blunt object, presumably the back side of an axe. We don't have the murder weapon yet, but we'll find it. As soon as we blow up the ice on Long Lake, we'll find it. Most

171

killers prefer the blunt side of the axe, for when one uses the sharp side one cracks open the head, like this—he dragged his finger over his smooth skull—one splits it, so to speak, and *sees* the hell one is creating. Even in the most violent state of anger, all murderers are aware of this. Which would you have chosen, Jon, the blunt edge or the sharp one?"

Jon would have chosen the blunt edge.

"Yes, the blunt one."

"It doesn't especially bother you to talk about it, does it?"

"Uh . . . yes, it does."

"It just *seems* not to?"

He gave no answer.

"So we have to look elsewhere. Let's say that I have three motives—three *probable* motives—and approximately the same number of suspects. Then you bring up yet another: money, of all things! But you certainly have money, Jon, isn't that right?"

"No."

"But you *had* money before you used it up on the new wall. Why didn't Lisa come to you?"

"I don't know."

"That same evening you sat at Karl's, drinking. There, too, the conversation had to do with money. Are you stingy?"

No, it was Karl who was stingy. Besides, they didn't quarrel about money *that* evening.

Hermansen thundered on relentlessly.

"Lisa knew that you were willing to cut off your right arm at her slightest suggestion, yet she first badgers her father and two cast-off lovers. What happened at Karl's that evening?"

"I don't remember!"

"But that you didn't quarrel about money—you *do* remember that?"

"Yes, because I remember *when* we quarreled about money. It was later in the fall, when he was digging potatoes."

172

"It's a good thing for you that he doesn't remember anything, isn't it?"

"Yes."

They looked at each other. "No," said Jon. "I don't know. You destroy everything."

Hermansen said, "Lisa came to Karl that evening. She *knew* that you and he were sitting there because you had told her about it earlier in the day. For there are witnesses to the fact that you and she *did* have contact with each other last summer."

"There are not."

"How else would you know about the money?"

"She wrote to me."

"Ha!"

Hermansen paused, then continued.

"I said that there are several suspects, each with a plausible motive. But it is also possible to attribute all of the motives to one person: you. That would explain the paradoxical behavior you have exhibited in recent months. You conceal even as you try to reveal."

"I don't understand what you mean."

"Yes you do. What were you doing, for example, outside Sakkariassen's windows at night?"

That was a difficult question. And if it was clear to Hermansen, for Jon it was shrouded in fog. He thought vaguely that when the old man lost interest in everything, both the new water and the fish works, it was not because he was getting old, like Nils, but because he realized that something had happened to Lisa. Maybe Jon wanted to find out what he knew, as they had talked about the day before. It was impossible to give any answer.

"Who was the witness?" he asked.

"Elisabeth."

"That's not true."

"You have too many things to keep track of, Jon. You're getting all mixed up. You always end up pointing at yourself."

173

"I haven't done anything."

"I'm no big sister, Jon. I'm no well-intentioned teacher or drunken neighbor who feels sorry for you. I'm going to keep after you until you crack."

"Now something is happening," said Jon. He was referring to the weather. The man in the orange coveralls came back and said that the road was open. They could drive on—carefully.

21

Jon didn't believe in God. Not because he had rational scruples, but because the Lord was so unpredictable. He believed in that which he considered good and in that which he desired. Elisabeth believed in love, Hans in politics and the new water. What did Hermansen believe in? Jon didn't know. He didn't understand that type of person. They assembled various little pieces of the world and no doubt were happy when they could combine them into a comprehensible picture. Maybe he was driven by a sense of justice—but then, so was everyone else, including Elisabeth and Hans. Maybe he hated someone, just as Jon hated Sakkariassen. Or maybe he was just doing his job.

"Listen," said Hermansen as he read the same weather report for the tenth time. "Two inches of precipitation, and you claim it was sunny?"

They were talking about Saturday the 27th of August again.

"It *was* sunny," said Jon.

"Elisabeth says that you and Lisa left the house about 11 A.M. and walked northward toward the fish works. Sakkariassen says that she got there a little after three. Isn't that a long time?"

Four hours out on the heath with Lisa? Why, that was hardly any time at all.

"In *that* weather?"

"What about it?"

"What did you do during those four hours?"

Jon laughed.

"You made plans together, didn't you?"

"No."

"In any case, you split up before she got to the fish works, because nobody there saw you. She packed up, and in the evening she took a southbound bus, presumably intending to go away. Instead she looked up Hans and asked for money."

This business about the money was really a crucial point. Hermansen included it or omitted it to suit whatever he was saying, and Jon had not been able to find out what Hans had said during the snowstorm when they were waiting for the road to clear.

"From there she went to the party at the community house to talk with Georg."

At this point Hermansen dropped Lisa and began talking about Jon.

Jon had come home after the long visit to the heath, had eaten dinner with Elisabeth, and then had gone to Karl's to help him slaughter a calf—which was another crucial point, for wasn't August much too early for slaughtering? And did anyone do their own slaughtering any more? This was something Jon had never bothered to try to clear up, so Hermansen must have confirmed it in some other way—for they *had* slaughtered on the 27th of August. Afterward they drank, which he knew not because he remembered it—and Margrete had gone to a meeting of the party committee at the community house—but because they always drank when they finished slaughtering. They quarreled, then drank some more, and the hours went by and vanished in drunkenness and oblivion.

And Jon was not the only one who had no memory of this fateful night. Elisabeth, Hans, Karl, the divers—none of them could recount anything of interest. Hermansen even mumbled something about a collective feeling of guilt and repression.

Jon thought about the telephone conversation he had had with his sister the previous evening. She was in an empty new flat, which made her voice echo, and she was trying to sound like the protective big sister and at the same time to excuse her sudden departure. It didn't work.

"I've sent you a package," she said when the conversation broke down completely. "Have you gotten it?"

"No."

He had gotten just one Christmas gift this year—jogging shoes from Hermansen, so they could go running in the evenings and have a little fun together.

"Well, I'm sure it'll come soon. Oof, how are things going with you, Jon? Are you really not allowed to tell anything?"

Allowed or not, he had nothing to tell.

"Well, is he just standing there and looking after you, then?"

"Not exactly."

"He didn't tell me a thing. Just asked a bunch of questions. But he was quite nice. Do you like him?"

"Yes."

"So he's not badgering you?"

"No."

"Well, that's good. It's just a preliminary hearing, you know. You're a witness, he said."

"Yes, no doubt."

She told him about the new school, about the moving van that got stuck in Christmas traffic and couldn't move. Then she fell apart completely.

"Poor boy," she cried hysterically. "What have you done? We can't go on like this, Jon—at least not now. You must tell it. You must!"

He didn't know what she meant.

"I'm not lying," he said.

"Haven't you seen what they are writing about you in the newspapers? O God, it's awful!"

He knew that there had been something, but Hermansen had refused to let him read it.

"I haven't done anything," he said.

She couldn't talk any more, and the conversation ended in tears. Jon realized that something in his life was gone for good—something he wanted to hang on to. He had seen it in the faces of the islanders, heard it in Elisabeth's voice. The same realization was confirmed when he reviewed his videos. Hermansen had gotten them all together, and they sat hour after hour in front of the TV watching the dedication of the new water with the mayor and Rimstad, Hans being interviewed with a whiny son on his shoulders, Georg in his diving outfit, Marit and Elisabeth, Margrete prancing around on the stoop, Lisa's funeral with Sakkariassen in tears, and hours of nothing—just the wall in the living room at home with Jon half asleep in a chair in front of the camera. It was all in the past, the distant past, and as laughable as declarations of love in an album from one's school days.

"This just gets worse and worse," barked Hermansen. No doubt he had expected something or other of value to emerge from so many videotapes. "Why in the world did you buy that camera?"

"To remember better."

"Ha ha."

Only once did a picture arouse the policeman's interest.

"Who is that?" he shouted, stopping the film.

It was Elisabeth dressed in oilskins out in the yard of their home. The rain was pouring down, a lock of hair hung out of the hood and stuck to the rubber. Elisabeth as she was before Hans and the big disappointments, in Jon's oversized oilskins one day when he had persuaded her to go fishing with him out in the ocean.

"Elisabeth."

"Are you sure?"

"Who else could it be?"

"I don't know. Lisa, maybe."

He was right up by the screen.

178

"No, it's Elisabeth."

"Well, if you say so."

Hermansen was beginning to show signs of weakness. So it appeared, at least, to Jon, perhaps because his own fear had been gone for awhile.

Two sheets of paper were placed on the table, with big circles covered by innumerable dots in various colors that at first seemed to have no pattern. But when you looked more closely, a number—23—emerged in one circle, and a letter—B—in the other. Jon was not colorblind, nor did he allow himself to be confused by the other perception tests that he was compelled to take.

"We're getting close," said Hermansen, but he didn't sound convincing. New points were brought up less and less often. The sheets of paper had become dog-eared, and the policeman's armpits stank. When the interrogation first began he had been surrounded by assistants who came in with new papers or to tell him that he had to take a telephone call in the next room—strong young men who followed Jon when he went on walks in the city and shook the curtain if he stayed too long in the shower. Now most of them had left, and in that connection Jon had overheard a conversation in the lobby during which Hermansen shook his head and said that what he was doing was a balancing act between two concepts that he—Jon—didn't understand.

And that surprised him. If everyone was convinced that he had killed Lisa, why didn't they convict him and send him to prison like they were supposed to?

A couple of days before New Year's Eve, Hermansen, after a long period of silence, stood up and left to take a shower. He took his time, and when he returned he was wearing a new shirt. He put on his jacket and knotted his tie. His desk top was no longer chaotic. The papers that remained were filed in neatly labelled folders.

There was no pen and no typewriter, for now there was to be neither reading nor writing.

"When Lisa left the community house, she went to Karl's, where you and he sat drinking."

"Could be," said Jon.

"Don't get smart with me, Jon."

"I won't."

They had been through all of this countless times and Jon had given the same answer each time.

"She told you about the unsuccessful appeals to Hans and the divers. You and she went to your house to make some plans. Elisabeth was gone, so you had the house to yourselves. Some time during the night you left the house and went out to Long Lake." He hesitated. "That her clothes were found under the stone on North Island obviously means only that you put them there, not that she was killed there. Uh . . . I assume that she deceived you again."

Jon said, also for the umpteenth time, that Lisa had never deceived him. Nor had he ever deceived her. They had been unlucky, constantly subjected to pressure from their surroundings as they were. But they had never deceived each other. They were the right and left arms of the same body.

"There was light in the crew shed when you got to Long Lake, so you knew the divers were back from the party. Lisa asked you to wait outside while she went in and talked to them. You waited. But she didn't come out again. You had tolerated her duplicity before— once, twice, God knows how many times—because she always managed to win you over one way or another. She was smart, and she was a woman. But this time it was too much for you. She had led you to think that she wanted to move back to the island, to you. You and she would realize your common dream, an eternal childhood, romantic and undisturbed, once you got Elisabeth out of the house. Am I right?"

These last assumptions were new. According to this version, there was a fight with the divers and Lisa was killed by accident.

Jon observed his own reaction as if from outside himself. He felt no flush of anger over what he heard, no tenseness in his body. His hands lay calmly on the arm rests, and his eyes shone with the confidence of one who is satisfied with himself.

"But you forgot that Lisa was no longer a child like you. These were no longer her dreams, just yours. She had been out in the world and had lost her dreams. She deceived you one more time with that wretched diver."

Jon observed that Hermansen didn't like what he was doing, and he started to laugh. Hermansen saw this, and even looked embarrassed.

"You sat and waited until she came out again. Then you had only to *look* at her to understand that everything you had believed in and dreamed of was nothing but laughable nonsense. She had destroyed it, every last shred of it, and only by destroying *her*—as she was *then*—could the dream survive."

He drew a deep breath and continued.

"It was not about money. That was just something she told you. She wanted to go to Long Lake that night to see Georg. He had rejected her, and she couldn't tolerate that. Jon, your picture of her as an innocent and impulsive child is a cliché. She took you along for the company, not to help her get money from the divers. Maybe for a little solace along the way, for it can be boring to walk all that way alone. Ever since she had her first affair with Hans you were nothing but a clown to her."

When someone acted friendly toward Jon during his school days it made him feel uneasy, and he immediately demanded that the person in question say what he *really* thought of him—namely, that Jon didn't deserve friendliness, that he deserved only contempt and condescension. That was much easier to deal with than the complicated perils inherent in a friendship. No such demand was necessary in Hermansen's case.

"It was a shock for you to realize what you had done. You lost your memory and couldn't put all the pieces together. But they kept

181

popping up anyway, in various situations, and you had to put them into a pattern that you could live with. You wanted to depict her father as a murderer, or at least as the one who was truly responsible for Lisa's destruction and, consequently, for what happened at Long Lake. You tried the same thing with Hans when you began to realize that your stories didn't hang together, then with the divers—everyone that you thought was to blame for Lisa's fall."

Hermansen stopped, and Jon noticed that his shiny pate was glistening with sweat. His eyes no longer looked balanced and resolute. It appeared as if he were uncomfortable, restlessly waiting, presumably in the hope that Jon's reaction would carry the conversation forward. But Jon showed no reaction at all.

"I'm not the one who did it," he said.

"You won't give me any details?"

"I'm not in jail. If I had done it I would be in jail."

Hermansen folded his white hands and looked at the floor.

"I've been treating you like a normal person," he said, "even though the community insisted that you're crazy. I see now that I was wrong. Let's go over the whole matter from the beginning."

22

It was five o'clock in the morning, and the whole town was asleep. The harbor lay still beneath the falling snow. Jon, standing at the window, saw a truck park in front of the hotel entrance and unload steaming cases of fresh bread onto the sidewalk.

Only one car was in the parking lot, and footprints led from it down past the warehouses to the harbor. The same car had stood there every snowy morning since he had come here. The footprints were those of the skipper of the boat that delivered goods and passengers to the outlying islands.

Jon got dressed and left the room. He didn't meet anyone in the corridor or on the stairs. The lobby was also empty. He emerged unseen out into the biting cold, followed the footprints down to the wharf, and boarded the waiting boat.

He spent two uncomfortable hours shivering in his hiding place under the foredeck until, stiff and sore, he went ashore on his island.

The road was covered with deep snow. Everything was covered with deep snow. It was a community in hibernation.

The house was like an empty skull, with bare walls and dark windows, cold and empty, as if to conceal a hideous crime. Only his armchair remained, standing forlornly on the carpetless floor—the tattered old relic from his father's glory days as foreman of the seining crew.

He put wood and coal in both fireplaces and started them burning. He emptied the fuel-oil tank in the cellar and splashed the flammable liquid all over the floor and the walls in the living room and the kitchen. Then he sat down in the armchair, holding the matches in his hand. He had come home to wind things up once and for all.

But it was natural to wait a little while. He had no pressing thoughts to think through, nothing to confess or settle with himself, no angst to come to grips with. It just seemed natural to wait a little while.

He was awakened by sounds out in the yard, stomping feet, and someone calling his name. It was light outside, and he realized that he had been sleeping quite awhile.

Hermansen came into the house. A look as intense and unreal as the first time they met, a stranger who sniffed the oil smell but said nothing. He was wearing a long, off-white raincoat, but no hat, and snow clung to his legs all the way to the knees. The mixture of melted snow and fuel oil made a squishing sound as he walked across the floor.

"The road was snowed in," he said offhandedly. He sat down on the floor in the driest corner he could find, but still the oil and water stained his coat. He noticed it but paid no attention to it.

Jon nodded impatiently toward the matches.

"I'm going to light it," he said. "You have to leave."

"And you?" asked Hermansen. "Will you leave?"

"No."

"Then neither will I."

Jon laughed. This heroism seemed as meaningless to him as everything else this busybody squirrel had gathered and garbled with his logical understanding. He didn't believe him. He had not spoken a true word during the entire time they had known each other. His whole being was directed toward one goal: to get Jon to confess to something he hadn't done. He had called him a Peeping Tom and a deranged snooper, was condescending when he did accept what Jon said, had taken turns being nice and being threatening.

No doubt the house was surrounded by cops—just as there was no doubt that the feigned self-control on the face in the corner concealed profound anxiety. They were sitting on a bomb.

"I'm going to light it," he shouted. "You'll be killed!"

"You've had several hours," Hermansen said. "You could have lit it before."

Jon opened the box, took out a match, lit it, and threw it on the floor. It went out. He struck a second match. It also went out. He ripped a piece of wallpaper off the wall and set fire to it.

Hermansen leaped to his feet. The smugness had disappeared. "Stay where you are!" said Jon. He held the burning wallpaper in one hand and the matches in the other, and he seethed with contempt. Nothing smelled as bad as power turned to weakness. "Sit down!" he bellowed.

Slowly, tensely, Hermansen sank back to the floor—to his knees, like a sprinter in the starting position. His cheeks and his forehead were white.

"Why do you think she had those coveralls on?" Jon shouted. "And my sweater?"

"There are many questions regarding this matter that only you can answer, Jon," he said. "But that doesn't make you innocent."

Jon snorted. He had confessed to illegal acts before and had messed up the whole pattern of his life. There was never any connection between crime and punishment. For when he did something, be it lawful or otherwise, it was to correct an imbalance, to defend himself, or to supply something that was lacking. He was not an evil person, one who destroys simply for the sake of destroying.

"You don't even have anything to attack me with," he said contemptuously.

"That's why I let you go," said Hermansen. Jon thought he detected that the policeman's self-confidence was beginning to return. "Without the murder weapon there isn't much we can do."

Jon laughed. More lies. And new tricks.

Suddenly the flames reached his fingers, and he shook the piece of wallpaper vigorously. Hermansen was on him in a flash.

"Don't hit me!" Jon whimpered meekly, huddling down to protect himself. Hermansen checked the blow at the last instant, at once angry and relieved, grabbed the matches and opened the box.

Then Jon struck. Just as Hermansen was savoring his triumph, with all the strength and force he could muster Jon sent a crushing blow to the policeman's face. He fell to the floor with a loud thump, and long before he came to Jon had pushed him back into the corner, picked up the matches, and ignited another piece of wallpaper—a much bigger one this time.

Hermansen could only mumble. "I must be getting old," he said.

He wiped the blood off his face and neck. His breath came in labored gasps between his words. "No, I don't know why she was wearing the coveralls and your sweater, but I can try to guess. It's possible that she didn't go to Karl's that evening, that she went straight to Long Lake. It rained cats and dogs all night, and she was soaking wet when she got there. She hung up her own clothes in the crew shed to dry and borrowed one of Georg's coveralls while she was waiting. At the same time, you left Karl's and went to the community center to look for her, for you and she had agreed that you were going to hit up the divers for some money. When you didn't find her there, you realized that she had gone to Long Lake. You went there, found her in the crew shed—obviously it wasn't exactly *you* she had been waiting for—and you sat and talked. She was cold and borrowed your sweater."

Jon said, "Why did you let me go?"

"So that when you came here . . ."

He was finding it hard to talk. Jon laughed.

"Then I would confess?"

"No, not that. But . . . something could happen."

"What, then?"

Hermansen gave no answer.

"You think I'm nice," Jon said mockingly. "You're just like Elisabeth, like Hans and all the others. You don't understand anything. *She was wearing the coveralls so she wouldn't be naked!*"

"Naked?"

"Yes, naked!"

"*That's* why you put clothes on her before you sank her in the lake?"

Jon did not respond to that. He had not killed Lisa. Everyone else had done that. He had protected her against misuse and dishonor. For one fleeting moment, perhaps, he felt a desire to correct the reasoning of this uncomprehending policeman, to enlighten him, to hold the real truth up before his eyes and shatter that idiotic self-confidence. But he had never gotten anywhere with his explanations in the past, and he was neither a rabble-rouser nor a teacher. He just hadn't wanted everybody to see Lisa naked. It was as simple as that. And yet it was completely incomprehensible to this educated idiot.

"Was *that* important?" asked Hermansen. "What about life itself, then?"

Life? Perhaps it was fine once upon a time, but now it was trash. It had all disappeared—childhood, the summers, his mother, Elisabeth, home. They all slipped willy-nilly through his fingers, no matter what he did to hold on to them. What happened at Long Lake was nothing but a simple little rescue operation, the preservation of the *only* thing that could not die.

"So the divers never had anything to do with it?" asked Hermansen. "Georg was telling the truth when he said he saw her for the last time at the party?"

Jon didn't know anything about that. And Hermansen gave the impression that he was bewildered. He shook his head and started to say something, then suddenly stopped, maybe because talking made his mouth hurt. He stood up and let his hands hang limply at

187

his side to signal that he would make no further attempts to over-power Jon.

"Go," said Jon.

"And you? What are you going to do?"

He wasn't going to do anything.

"I'll be here," he said. "That's all."

The east wind was flinging dry snow against the windows. Hermansen rubbed his bald scalp distractedly, tramped around in the pools of oil, but still did not leave.

"You're not going to light it?" he said. "You—"

Jon stopped him with a cold laugh.

"No," he said. "I just want to be alone."

"Then you will tell me what happened?"

"Afterwards."

He drew a deep breath. "There are others outside the house," he said. "Tell them to go with you."

He backed into the wettest corner, far away from the windows and the unpredictable Hermansen. The piece of wallpaper he had been holding was all burnt up. He tore off another piece and lit it.

"Go," he said again.

Hermansen hesitated. He looked at the floor, looked at Jon, made a decision and went.

Jon waited until the footsteps reached the front stoop and the outside door had slammed shut. Then he closed the inner door and turned the key. Outside he saw the back of Hermansen's white coat and his slow, halting course down toward the birch grove. His shoulders were elevated, and he clutched the oil-stained coat tightly about him to ward off the biting wind. Even now he was not an old man on his way home, just the same incurable optimist.

Jon thought of Lisa and looked at his hands. They were not shak-ing. He dropped the burning paper. He saw the flames sweep like a wave of blue water over to the walls, saw them strike the ceiling in powerful yellow gusts. He felt no pain. He knew what would hap-pen if he now went to the kitchen and put on his jacket, if he pulled

188

a cap down over his crackling hair and walked out into the cold and the wind. He would put the past firmly behind him and be taken into custody by Hermansen and the other men who at this very moment were pounding the walls and breaking the windows in a futile attempt to get him out. Hermansen would drop to his knees and rub snow on his burning trousers to put out the fire. Over the policeman's broad, oil-spattered back he would see his childhood home filled with crackling flames that spread to the second floor, then to the attic, and that finally burst through the roof to become one with the howling wind.

Through the birch grove he would see the turquoise-blue sea, the fishing fleet tied up at the moorings, perhaps a coastal freighter pulling in to the wharf.

"I'm freezing," he would think to himself. "I'm freezing."

About the Author

Roy Jacobsen (b. 1954) has been called the *wunderkind* of contemporary Norwegian literature. His first book, *Prison Life (Fangeliv,* 1982)—a collection of short stories—was soon followed by several novels, a children's book, and a second collection of short stories. *The New Water (Det nye vannet,* 1987) was the work that established Jacobsen's reputation in Norway as a writer of exceptional talent and psychological depth. The author's many honors include the Tarjei Vesaas Prize for Best First Publication (1982), the Cappelen Prize (1987), the Notabene Prize (1988), the Association of Norwegian Literary Critics' Prize (1989), and The Bookseller Prize (1991).

The New Water is the first of Jacobsen's books to appear in English.